A Street King To Love

by

Jamie Marie

Synopsis

There comes a moment in everyone's life when you have to decide who is most worthy of love others or yourself, first. For young My'Zariah Preston, she has never quite learned that lesson but as she gets older, the universe keeps trying to teach her a very important life lesson. After being in a relationship for over two years, My'Zariah is now suspecting that everything she suspected is the furthest from the truth. She's not the only one learning new truths, either.

Keon Preston, My'Zariah's older brother, has always been open when it comes to his sexuality but his on and off again boyfriend, on the other hand, is the complete opposite. Will Keon love himself enough to know he's worth more than being someone's little secret?

Jadarius White has always been a workaholic. Before, it was in the streets but now he's reformed and prefers to get his money the legal way. Too busy for love, JD has never even expressed interest in a woman, but My'Zariah is different. After a while, he'll discover how different she actually is. Will he be able to handle it?

My'Zariah "Mizzy" Preston

The sounds of "Don't Say Goodnight" by the l Isley Brothers could be heard all throughout the banquet hall as everyone in the building watched as my grandparents danced to their song. The lights were dimly lit as they danced under the spotlight. This was the song they had at their wedding thirty years ago. It was only right that they shared the first dance of the night to celebrate Thirty years of marriage to this song. I looked on in complete awe as they looked into each other's eyes and sang to each other. I couldn't help but shed a tear as I watched, It was something straight out of a fairytale. Everyone knew my grandparents were my life. They raised me from an infant when my mother left me.

My mother was only sixteen when I was born, and she was too caught up in life to have anything to do with me at that time. She wasn't even one hundred percent sure who my father was. The boy she tried to pin me on had a DNA test done, which, of course, came back he wasn't my father. Instead of staying to raise me, my mother decided to skip

town, leaving me in the care of my grandparents. They took
on the responsibility of another child while still raising
kids. At the time my mother abandoned me, she had two
younger brothers and a younger sister, who were minors.
My grandparents never treated me any differently from the
other kids. I just became one of theirs. Although my mother
was now in the picture whenever she felt like it, our
relationship was strained. I never looked at her as a parent,
but like a big cousin. I couldn't even say sibling. My
grandparents's other kids were who I considered my
brothers and sister.

"Mizzy, I know you not over here crying like some big ass
kid. Wipe those tears, you know Mama and Daddy don't
want you over here crying like this."

I looked over at my "brother," Keon, who was stuffing his
face with lemon pepper chicken bites and meatballs. Keon
was the youngest boy and was only a few years older than
me, and out of all of us, we got along the best. We were
each other's diary. Whenever either of us had men
problems, we went to each other to talk about it. It seemed
like no one understood us but each other. He was really my
best friend in this crazy ass world.

"Ke, I can't help but to cry. Look how happy they are. They
look so adorable dancing and gazing at one another."

"I know, girl. Mama and Daddy look so good together.
Definitely the poster for true Black love."

2

"Yes! Definitely. I still can't believe we actually planned this and it came out perfect. I can't wait to finish school so I can really get my event company up and running."

"Yes, my sister, so you can plan me and my future husband's wedding in a few years."

"Keon, you need a man first. You can't keep one 'cause you are so extra and always scaring them off. So how you standing up here, talking about a wedding?"

If looks could kill, I would be a dead woman because I couldn't help but laugh at the look Ke gave me. Keon was openly gay and very feminine, down to his nails and hair and the way he would sometimes dress. He still wore men's clothing, but for special occasions, like tonight, he was decked out in a pair of black, ripped skinny jeans from Fashion Nova and paired with a cream-colored sweater that hugged his body right. On his feet were a pair of bad ass YSL, six-inch, black boots. His nails were freshly done in his signature French manicure. He didn't wear much jewelry, just a pair of diamond studs that shined so brightly under the dim lights. His locs were freshly re-twisted and styled neatly with the tips dyed blonde. My brother looked the fuck good, but right now, he was giving me the death stare.

"Bitch, don't you come for me and my man. I don't run them off, they just don't know how to handle me. And for your information, Malik and I are doing just fine. He is the

3

only man that matters. He will be my husband, so get ready
to plan the wedding of the decade."

"And where is Malik tonight, since he is your future
husband?"

"He had to work. Don't worry about my man, where is
Ryan at tonight?"

"Screw that nigga. He couldn't even take an hour or two to
come out with me tonight, talking about he was busy. It
would have been OK if I just sprung this on him a few days
ago but he knew this shit for a few months. He could have
planned better. His ass probably out there, doing only God
knows what, but if I catch his ass, I'm gon' slice and dice
his ass."

"Sounds like you're the one with the man problems, Mizzy,
not me. I think it's time we plan a weekend, just the two of
us. We can fly down to Tennessee in the mountains and do
some shopping. How does that sound?"

"Yeah, Keon, I think I need to get out of Charlotte for a
while, just to clear my head. I have been so busy with
school and planning different events, I haven't had any
time to myself. I am honestly shocked I was able to pull
this off for Mama and Daddy."

"OK, cool, so in the next few days, we will get together and go over our schedules and plan a weekend. But tonight, let's enjoy this beautiful night you put together for Mama and Daddy."

I gave Keon a big hug because he really knew how to make me feel better. I was a little pissed about Ryan not even making an effort to try to come tonight. I loved my man, but our relationship was really in a different place at the moment. I often thought it was because of me working and going to school, but I didn't know. Hopefully, we can figure us out.

"Well, honeybun, I hate to ruin this sentimental moment between us, but here comes your biological mammy."

"Ahh, shit. The fuck does she want, man? I just want a smooth night with no issues. I don't even know why they invited her ass."

"Be nice, Mizzy, she is still your mama."

"No, the lady on that dance floor is my mama. Mellissa just pushed me out."

The way my birth mother walked through the building, hugging and laughing with everyone, was sickening to me. She really walked around like she didn't dump a child off on my grandparents and leave without a care in the world.

No one could deny how beautiful she was and I was a spitting image of her from the honey blonde skin, hazel eyes, and even deep dimples. We even had the same curl pattern in our natural hair. Tonight, she wore her beautiful hair in a natural, messy bun with little curls framing her face. She was a work of art in so many ways. I watched as she strutted her way over to where Keon and I were standing, and I had to have a mental talk with myself to remain calm and remember tonight was all about my grandparents.

"Look at my baby girl and my baby brother. Y'all look so good tonight. My'Zariah, you did a wonderful job with the decorations and everything. I'm so proud of you, baby."

"Thank you, Mellissa, anything for Mama and Daddy."

I looked over at Keon, who was giving me the death stare again because he knew my last statement was out of pure pettiness, but I didn't care one bit how she felt. I hated she was even invited, but it made my grandmother happy, so here we were.

"How long are you in town for, Mellissa?" I questioned my birth mother out of curiosity, not really caring.

"I might stay for a while, spend some time with my family and my daughter."

"What daughter? Me? I know you high or something 'cause ain't no way in hell you trying to spend time with me. You twenty years too late for that. Try again."

"Mizzy!"

"Don't Mizzy me, the fuck. I'm going over there with my parents that raised me, if you would excuse me."

Lord knows I wasn't trying to be rude or disrespectful, but she had me fucked up, talking about she wanted to spend time with her daughter. I swear I tried to be cordial around Mellissa, but sometimes, her presence alone took me to a dark place. A place I did not need or want to be anymore.

I had been going to therapy for a while and I knew too much time with her would lead me to more sessions.

The place was beginning to get packed and I needed to get my camera ready to start taking pictures for the evening. Walking out to my car, the cool breeze from the southern fall weather was a welcome to my skin. I was starting to feel a little hot in the building since it was now completely full.

I hit the lock on my 2022 Honda Accord to unlock the
doors and grab my camera and tripod. I wanted to get
family photos, but also shots of everyone enjoying the
party. I quickly grabbed my things and rushed back inside.
I didn't like being out there all alone; shit happened so fast
in Charlotte.

I tried calling Ryan just to see what he was doing and try to
convince him to come out for a while, but just as I
expected, the call went straight to voicemail. That female
intuition started to tingle, and I got a bad feeling that he
was out there doing shit he had no business doing. I just
prayed for his sake he wasn't.

I made it back inside the building and saw my other
"siblings," Kelsey and Romelo, along with Keon on the
dance floor with my grandparents. Everyone looked so
happy and it really made me smile that I was able to do this
for them.

For the rest of the night, I walked around, taking pics and
dancing with my grandparents. The later it got, the more I
wished my boyfriend, Ryan, could have been here with me.
It really bothered me he couldn't take a few hours to come
with me tonight. I was always going out of my way for
him, but the same couldn't be done for me. Him and
anyone else was in for a very rude awakening because I
was getting fed up with being played with and a change
was coming soon and very soon.

Keon "Ke" Preston

I was so glad to finally be on my way home from my parents's anniversary party. Mizzy did such an amazing job with the event. My baby sister knew she was too talented to not take her event business to the next level. As long as there was breath in my body, I would be her biggest cheerleader every step of the way.

Out of all of us, Mizzy and I were the closest; we practically grew up together. We were only two years apart. She was the first person I came out to and, unlike everyone else, she never judged me or tried to change me. She let me be myself around her. My other siblings were ashamed of me, at first, but they all eventually came around. I even dressed them for their proms and other events.

I was a badass makeup artist and was currently growing my clientele with the help of Mizzy and all of her connections with modeling agencies in Charlotte. I even had a gig tomorrow to do makeup for swimsuit models for one of the local sports magazines and I was too excited.

Now, though, I was ready to go see my man. He sent me a text, letting me know he had made it to my house. Although Malik and I broke up once a month, he was honestly my everything and the one man who truly had my heart. What we had was complicated but it was true love. Malik wasn't completely out of the closet, and that was really the only reason we argued. I wanted him to let the world know I was his man, but just like my family at first, his family wouldn't be supportive of his relationship with me. I always reassured him I loved him, no matter what. However, I wasn't the type of bitch you kept hidden—I was a bitch you showed off.

I made it to my condo and hit the engine on my Nissan Maxima. Malik's GMC Denali was parked in the visitor spot next to my spot. Thankfully, I didn't have much to carry, only my Telfar bag and keys. Opening the door to my condo, the smell of weed hit me like a blow to the nose. Whatever my man was smoking, that shit was strong. I was not a big smoker, but I could tell that was some good shit.

"What's up, baby? How was the party?" Malik's deep, raspy voice always sent a chill down my spine. Not in a fearful way, but in a sexual way. I loved this man with everything and I went to bed every night, praying for him and our relationship. Many nights, I dreamed of the day we could walk in public, hand in hand. Don't get me wrong, we went on dates, but we never showed affection.

"It was good. I had to stop Mizzy from going off on Mellissa. You know how short her temper is. Other than that, it was nice. Mizzy did a great job with everything, but you would have known that if you came."

"Bae, why you gotta go there? I told you I had some shit to handle. Don't start that shit, Keon."

"How am I starting? I just answered your question."

"Yeah, OK."

The last thing I wanted to do was start an argument, but I was in a mood. Malik never hesitated to ask me about my day or night. He really was the sweetest man ever. I just wished he would get over his fear.

Walking over to where Malik was sitting, I sat down on his lap and hugged his neck as he passed me the blunt, allowing me to take a long pull before I passed it back to him. I blew out a few rings of smoke and watched as they disappeared in the air. Closing my eyes and tilting my head back, I let the weed relax me. If only for a moment, I was in another dimension as the good herb took over.

"I'm sorry, Malik. I didn't mean to come off like I did, baby, but you know how I feel."

"And you know how I feel. This shit ain't easy for me. Don't get me wrong, I love the fuck out of you. You're my best friend, plus more, and I want nothing more than to let everyone know what it is. I am not afraid of my sexuality, but I am afraid of what to expect when I do come out. Just like you, I am big on family, and I remember how you told me you felt when your siblings basically disowned you. And I know everything with y'all is cool, but I don't know if my family will be so understanding. I honestly think they suspect something, but they haven't acted on it. I just need a little more time, please."

"You know I am not going anywhere, Malik. I got your back and you know I do. Just know that if your family truly loves you, they will love you regardless of who you choose to date. It's not you that has the problem, it's them. If they can't love you for you, do they even love you?"

I left him with a lot to think about. For the rest of the night, I just laid on the couch with my man as we watched reruns of *The Fresh Prince of Bel-Air*. I knew I had seen every episode hundreds of times but *The Fresh Prince of Bel-Air* was my comfort show, and right now, I was comfortable with just me and my man.

Malik was an early bird, so I wasn't surprised when I woke up and he was already gone. I had a slightly stiff neck from sleeping on the couch with Malik all night. After a much-needed stretch, I made my way upstairs to my master bedroom to prepare for my shower. The scent of Malik's Tom Ford Tuscan Leather cologne was still lingering in the air. That was one of my favorite scents for my man to wear.

I grabbed everything I needed for my shower and made my way to the bathroom. I allowed the hot water to relax me as I mentally prepared for the day. I was about to be the makeup artist for professional models. I couldn't believe it still.

I knew today would be a long day, so as I showered, I put together an outfit in my head. I stayed in the shower another fifteen minutes before stepping out to get myself together. I needed music to get ready, so I grabbed my iPhone 13 so I could connect to the Apple Play on my TV. Once it was connected, I let SZA sing to me as I used my Coco Chanel lotion to rub my body down. I sang along loudly as SZA talked about killing her ex. This song really had me in a chokehold at the moment. Hell, the whole album had me stuck. It was on heavy rotation daily.

The pause in the music let me know someone was calling and interrupting my personal concert I was having. I was annoyed that I was being bothered, but when I saw it was my man calling, I instantly perked up.

"Hello," I sang into the phone, happy to hear from him since I didn't get to see him this morning before he left. Malik was a paralegal, so he would often have really early days. I understood, so I never nagged or complained.

"Hey, bae, you good?"

"Yeah, I am good, getting dressed."

13

"I bet you got that music loud as hell and singing even louder."

"You know me so well, boo. What you doing calling me, anyway? Shouldn't you be working on some cases?"

"Yeah, I should be, but I wanted to take a minute to tell you I made reservations for us tonight for dinner. I will text you the address and information, you just make sure you are there."

"Aww, boo, I will make sure I am there."

"Aight, bet. I love you, and I will see you tonight."

"I love you, too, Malik."

I disconnected the call and started the music back up with a big smile on my face. This was something different with Malik. Don't get me wrong, we had our date nights, but I was the one always planning shit for us. So, Malik taking the lead on this was new to me. My mind was already going crazy, trying to think of an outfit to wear tonight. I had to look good for our date night. Who was I kidding? I always looked good.

I finished getting dressed for the day and looked at myself once more in the mirror. My retwist and color still looked good and I had only put on a little lip gloss for my face. I didn't want to do too much because I would be on my feet most of the day. I had on a black and white Nike sweatsuit with a pair of panda Dunks. Even dressed down, I was fine and I knew it.

I made my way to the venue in work mode. I was about to be in my zone, and I was ready to make these women look beautiful. When I arrived in the parking lot, I was shocked to see a sign that said makeup artist. "Not me getting my own parking space." This shit was legit.

Like the true professional I was, I parked in my assigned spot, grabbed my suitcase that had all of my equipment and product, and walked to the studio. Walking in, I took a moment to look around. There were lights and cameras everywhere. I was truly in complete awe of this place. I just knew I was legit now.

"Hi, you must be Keon?"

At the sound of my name, I turned around and was face to face with the most handsome man I had ever laid eyes on. He looked like he could be a twin to the rapper Nas, but not as hardcore and thuggish, but more laid back and casual. He was dressed down in a pair of black 501 jeans that hung off his hips just a little and a red and black Michael Jordan Bulls jersey that fit him perfectly. The black Coach cross body bag was an added accessory that complemented the look. A simple Apple watch with a black band was all the jewelry he wore. Now, I would never say I was an expert in knowing if a man was gay or not, but the way he looked at me and licked his lips let me know he liked what he saw.

"Yes, I am. And you are?"

"Zakari, the photographer, but you can call me Kari."

"Nice to meet you, Kari. Where do you need me?"

"Follow me."

We walked further into the building until we got to a room that was set up like a dressing room, but I assumed this would be the actual makeup room. There were three chairs in front of a huge mirror with big lights at the top.

"Here is where you can set up. The girls should be here in about an hour, so you have time to set everything up. Do you need anything? Water? Coffee? We have fresh fruit in the back, along with Starbucks, so help yourself."

"No, I am good, but if I change my mind, I will find my way to the back. Thank you."

"OK, well, just let me know if you need anything. I will be right out there."

I wasn't usually a nervous bitch, but looking at this man had my palms sweating and shit. There was surely an attraction there, but this was work and I needed to get myself together.

When Kari left the room, I removed my Telfar bag and started unpacking my suitcase that held all of my makeup. It took me exactly forty-five minutes to unpack and set up everything. I decided to take out my phone and see if Malik had texted me the details of our dinner date, and he had. I was so excited that he was taking me to one of my favorite restaurants tonight. Now that I knew where we were going, I had an idea of what I wanted to wear. With a few minutes left before the models arrived, I wanted to FaceTime Mizzy to thank her once again for helping me secure this opportunity.

"You don't have to even say anything, Keon. I know he is fine, and you're welcome."

"Mizzy, what are you talking about, bitch?"

"Keon, I know you like the back of my hand. You were calling to tell me how fine Kari is, but bitch, I already know and he is not interested in me. I am not his type. I have the wrong parts."

I had to cover my mouth because I just knew they could hear how loud I was laughing on the other side of the door. This little sneaky bitch had set me up.

"How do you know you have the wrong parts for him, bitch?"

"Because he told me. I have known Kari for a few months. We go to school together and, just like you, he comes to me with his man problems. Or he used to, until they broke up."

"Well, bitch, you are just in everybody's business, huh?"

"I'm only in what they put me in."

"You really are something else, My'Zariah Preston. What

are you about to get into, anyway?

"Going over to Mama and Daddy's house. Mama said she needed to talk to me. I think Mellissa's stupid ass snitched on me and told her how I talked to her last night."

"Bitch, I know you lying. I know Mellissa's old, over grown ass didn't tell Mama on you."

"Think so 'cause Mama gave me that 'you know better' voice."

"Well, I told your stubborn ass not to be so mean, but you don't listen. Now you got to hear Mama. That's all on you, baby."

"It's all good, Ke. I'm not taking back what I said, so fuck it."

"Well, all right, stubborn ass. I love you and I will talk to you later. I gotta get to work."

"OK, Keon, text me later. Maybe we can go out tonight."

19

"Can't, honeybun, my man is taking me on a date. Love you, bye."

I quickly hung up the phone and placed it on do not disturb. Soon, I had my Bluetooth speaker turned on and connected to my phone as the girls came in. I put on my makeup smock and got ready to work.

Each girl needed two different looks for each shoot, which was a total of twelve different looks. To many, that may seem like a lot, but I was cut out for this.

I made sure that each model was flawless before they left my chair and they were all satisfied. Once the last girl was done and on her way to her last shot of the day, I wanted to walk out and take a look at the actual photoshoot. My eyes went in Kari's direction and just like I was a few minutes ago, he was in his zone. He looked like a true professional, the way he guided the models. As if he knew someone was watching him, he looked back at me and gave me a wink. My God, those dark eyes were hypnotizing. Immediately, I turned around and headed back to the makeup room to gather all of my things and head out. I did not want to get caught up in those eyes.

After grabbing my bag and phone, I was prepared to walk out and head home. Before I could make it out the door, I saw Zakari coming my way.

"Keon, I want to thank you for everything; you really had

those girls looking good. You made my job easy because I won't have to do a lot of editing. I would love to show you the final photos. Do you have a few minutes to come over and look at them with me?"

"I actually have plans in a few hours, so I need to run, but you should have my email and number. You can send them to me and I can look at them tonight."

"Aight, bet, will do. Would you be willing to work with me and my girls again? We have a few more shoots coming up and I need a makeup artist."

"Hell yeah, I would love to, just send me the details and the contracts and we can talk business."

"How about we meet up one day this week to discuss face to face? I don't like doing business over the phone and computer."

If I didn't know earlier, I damn sure knew now; this man was flirting with me. I was usually the one shooting my shot, but this here, this was different. I was not used to a man being so bold. The shit was kind of turning me on.

"Umm, yeah, that's cool. We can make plans to meet up next week. You got my number, just hit me up."

"Aight, cool. You have a good night."

Whew, I needed to get away from this man. I also needed to have a conversation with my little sister for not warning me of the temptation I would be facing. *Temptation is a motherfucker I tell ya.*

Jadarius (JD) White

"Why you leaving so soon, JD? We got time, checkout is not until eleven."

"Nah, you already know I ain't no pillow-talking nigga, shorty. I been here far too long, but I'll hit you up in a few days."

"Why you spend all this money for a room, if all you gon' do is fuck and leave? We can go to your house for that. You wasting money on rooms."

"That lil bit of money I spend on this room ain't putting a dent in my pockets, sweetheart. Plus, I don't let nobody

23

know where I lay my head at night."

"Oh! I'm just a nobody now? As many times as we done fucked around, I'm a nobody to you? JD, you got me fucked up. You should be trying to make me your woman. Ain't no other bitch gon' keep fucking with you like me."

"Nah, shorty, you got me fucked up. Don't act like you didn't know what it was from the start, lil mama. I have never given you any reason to think I would make you my girl. You gotta bring more to the table than pussy."

"You trying to call me a hoe, nigga?"

"I ain't trying to call you shit, but if the thong fits, wear that motherfucker."

"Fuck you, JD. It will be awhile before you sample this pussy again, no matter how much you beg for it."

"Nah, you got me confused with one of them other lame ass niggas you fucking. I don't gotta beg for shit. Remember, you gave up the pussy on the first night."

24

"Fuck you, JD. Lose my damn number."

"Yeah, aight, you drive safe now."

Now, I wasn't a heartless motherfucker, so I left a few bills on the stand before grabbing my things and heading out. Today was my last time fucking with that bitch. She was starting to get too comfortable. She knew she was just a fuck from the beginning. What I didn't have time for was a clingy ass female constantly nagging for dumb shit like attention. My plate was already full with my business and my hustle. Females were just added baggage.

Jumping into my 2022 Scat Cat, I headed in the direction of my house. I was expecting my little brother and one of his homeboys who worked with us over to discuss business. I chose to build my house about twenty minutes from Charlotte, in Lake Park. It was a quiet subdivision, perfect for me.

I grew up in the city, so when I got older, I knew the city was not where I wanted to be twenty-four seven. Despite my lifestyle, I still wanted to live a quiet life with no added stress or pressure. As you could tell, I was in the drug game, but I didn't just sell drugs. Myself, along with my father and uncles, run a drug empire. We do it all, from weed to pills and meth. So, with the shit I dealt with for a living, I needed a little bit of peace in my life.

A lot of folks, including my parents, always asked me why I had such a big house and property if it was just me and my answer was always the same. I liked my freedom. I didn't have to worry about coming home to a woman who had an instant attitude if I stayed out until four in the morning. I was free to come and go and do as I pleased.

I made it to my house about twenty minutes later and parked in my circular driveway. My other two cars were parked in the garage, along with my bike and slingshot. The fact that I could decide on what vehicle I wanted to drive every day was boss to me.

Making it in, I made sure to check all of my cameras before heading up to my master bedroom and bathroom. My master suite was definitely fit for a king. My California king sized bed was placed in the middle of the room where I had the perfect view of the morning sunrise. The walk-in closet was the size of a large guest room and was lined floor to ceiling with shoes and clothes. I had a shopping habit, and by the look of my closet, it was evident.

I turned on ESPN as I got prepared to shower before my brother showed up. Thirty minutes later, as I made my way back downstairs, I saw my little brother pulling up to my driveway. I used the remote on my phone to unlock the door, allowing them to come in.

"JD, where you at, nigga?"

"I'm right here. Why the fuck you yelling?"

"Because I'm not about to search this big ass house looking for you. Nigga, you living in a mini mansion; who going through here, searching for you?"

"What if I didn't answer? Then what?"

"I would have sat my ass down and waited until you came from playing hide and seek in this motherfucker."

"Boy, go to hell 'cause you would have been all through my shit looking for me." I had to laugh at the back and forth between me and my brother. The shit was funny how he always tried to play hard. Lil nigga was stuck to me like glue and ain't shit would ever change that. That didn't stop him from talking that big shit when people were around, though.

"Anyway, the fuck you want me to come way out here for? You live way out in the fucking woods. A nigga could bury a few bodies out here and nobody would know shit."

"That's how I like it. Ain't nobody coming out here to fuck with me. But anyway, let's talk business. How is shit going out there? Y'all ain't got no heat on y'all or nothing, do you?"

"Nah, big bro, we straight. You already know if it's a problem, I'm coming to you first."

"That's what I like to hear, lil brother. What about on your end, Ryan? How shit running out on the west end?"

"Same ole, same ole, JD. Product still going out and money still coming in."

"That's what's up. You still got plans to open your barber shop? If so, whenever you ready, let me know and we can talk business. I got a few places I'm trying to buy and flip into a few new spots. I know you ain't trying to hustle all your life; the goal will forever be hustle until it pays off. Don't do this shit forever."

"Nah, I don't plan to, JD." I nodded, not needing to say anything else about the situation. All I could do was try to keep my niggas on the right path, especially if they had bigger goals.

"Well, since you here, my nigga, I need you to tape me up. My ass out here wolfing and shit. I can't have that. I need to look like a boss at all times."

28

"Yeah, I got you on the cut." I chopped it up with Johntae and Ryan for a few more hours until they both decided to head out and hit one of the gentlemen's club for the night. I thought about joining them, but quickly decided against the idea. I wouldn't mind sliding in my pussy for the night, but truth be told, a nigga was tired as fuck, so my night would just be me watching sports highlights on ESPN. Even a street king needed to lay low and relax for a while.

My'Zariah "Mizzy" Preston

The sweet voice of Summer Walker could be heard all throughout my apartment. I was in the middle of getting ready to head to my grandparent's house. My grandmother called me early in the morning to tell me she needed to see me today and that it was important. Only one thing came to my mind and it had to be my birth mother going back and whining to her because of what I said to her. I wasn't taking shit back. I had so much anger toward Mellissa, I physically could not stomach being in the same room with her, so her telling me she was staying in town to spend time with me pissed me off so bad. What the fuck you want to spend time with me for? She still had it in her mind that I was some little girl, crying out for her mama. Truth be told, I never cried for her and never would. If it wasn't for my grandparents, I wouldn't have shit to say to her.

My alarm alerting me that someone was coming in my house distracted me from my thoughts. Looking up, I saw Ryan coming in to the house carrying two bags and a cup holder from Chick-fil-A. He really had the nerve to walk in here like he didn't stay out all night and didn't even have the balls to call me and tell me he wasn't coming home.

One look at Ryan and I couldn't help but be mesmerized by his smile and those deep dimples. There was no denying it; this man was fine and he knew he was fine. He had smooth, chocolate skin that was covered in tattoos from his neck to his knuckles. His locs were pulled up into a high bun with a few framing his face. The once blonde tips were now light brown. The line-up was crisp as fuck, so I knew he had done it himself. I loved when he wore his hair up but I loved it more when we were fucking and they hung in his face.

"What's up, bae? What's with the look? Looking like you ready to shoot my head off and shit."

"You come in here carrying food like you right. You couldn't find your way home last night, or you couldn't find a minute to call or text me that you wasn't coming? Let me guess, you stayed at your apartment again last night. The apartment that you only have for business and to cut hair?"

"Mizzy, come on, ma, don't start. You know what it is with me. Plus, you had your grandparents's party last night, so after I made my rounds, I went to my spot and crashed and shit."

"Ryan, how dumb do you think I am? What gutter bitch were you entertaining at your spot last night? Any other time you out late, you always come home, but for the last few months, you can seem to only find home the next day. You slacking, my boy, doing shit sloppy. If you gon' fuck up, at least be smart about it. The fuck you think I am?"

"Come here, ma. What's really wrong with you, huh? Look, I wasn't doing shit last night and I for damn sure wasn't with a bitch. I know you still mad with a nigga for not making it to the anniversary party last night, and I am sorry. I am sorry for not communicating with you, too, OK? You can't say a nigga wasn't thinking about you; I got you some food. I know how much you love Chick-fil-A. I even got the sauce you like and the mixed drink you always get. Cut a nigga some slack, ma."

Truth be told, I wasn't even mad with Ryan at the moment, but his lack of communication was just slack. This whole shit with Mellissa had me in my feelings and everyone was bound to get it. I really hated being in this head space. I couldn't wait to get up with Keon to plan this little weekend getaway. I needed to get away from Charlotte and the people in it.

"I apologize for coming off on you the way I did. My anger should not have been directed at you. However, I still feel you could have called me or something. Shit was foul and disrespectful on your part, and as a female, of course, I am going to think you were with a bitch when you don't communicate with me. You can't blame me for that 'cause if I did it, you would think I was with a nigga."

"Why didn't you just call me? Communication works both ways, you know?"

"You know what, you right. I should have texted you. I will remember that next time. I am going to finish getting ready so I can go. Thanks for the food."

With that, I grabbed my drink and food and went back into my room to finish getting ready. I was tired of putting my feelings to the side for everyone and no one even acknowledging how I felt. Shit was getting old, and I was fed up with it. For him to come out of his mouth and say I should have called him was just stupid, and I felt it was a coverup for what he was doing. I was born at night, but for damn sure not last night, so he could stand up there and think he was getting one up on me. It was cool, but I would definitely have the last laugh.

I couldn't say for sure he was with another woman but that didn't take away from the fact that the stunt he pulled was foul. For the moment, I was done with the conversation.

I finished eating the food Ryan bought me and got dressed for the day.

By the time I was finished getting dressed and walking out of the room, Ryan had made himself comfortable on the couch, playing NBA 2K on his PlayStation 5, looking like a sexy god. This man was just too damn fine.

"Come get your ass whooped in this game, Mizzy."

"Can't, gotta go handle some shit at my grandparents's house. Some shit I would rather not deal with, but it is what it is."

"Everything good? Your grandparents straight?"

"Yeah, everything is good. I cussed Mellissa out last night and I think she went snitching to my grandma like I'm a four-year-old and shit."

"Your mama? What did you say to her?"

"That's not my mama. She was talking about staying in Charlotte to spend time with me and I told her no the fuck she won't. She must be high if she thinks she spending time with me."

34

"Damn, bae, why are you so mean?"

"I'm not mean, but fuck her and her feelings. I'm not sparing her feelings. Did she think about me when she dropped me off and left me? No the fuck she didn't. So it is what it is with me and her. I'm leaving, I will text you later."

Not giving him a chance to say anything else, I grabbed my keys, phone, and bag and walked off. Things with me and Ryan were different. I could feel a change with us. I had mad love for Ryan, but I didn't trust him like I used to, and the shit actually tugged at my heart because we had spent two years trying to build our relationship. Ryan was my first everything, and the thought of us not working out had me in my feelings bad. I wasn't trying to be a bitch to him back there, but I had feelings, and my feelings were really hurt by his actions last night.

I drove the fifteen minute drive to my parents's house with so many thoughts going through my head. A few times, I thought about not even going, but I knew my grandma would be pissed and curse me out from A-Z if I didn't show up. I pulled into my grandparents's driveway blasting, "Nobody's Supposed to be Here" by Deborah Cox . Me thinking it was only going to be me and my grandma, I was surprised to not only see Mellissa's car but also

35

Romelo's and Kelsey's. The hell was this, some type of intervention? I took a deep breath, turned off my car, and got out. I cursed myself for not hitting the blunt I had rolled up in my bag. This was about to be some bullshit, I could just feel it. Damn, how I wish Keon was here.

"Ma!" I yelled for my grandmother when I walked into the foyer of the house. My grandparents were old school, so you had to take your shoes off at the front door. She even had one of those hanging racks to put your shoes in when you took them off.

I heard my siblings in the living room as I walked further into the foyer so I made that my first stop. Kelsey was laid out on the couch while Romelo was on the chair and they were watching an episode of *The Jamie Foxx Show*.

"What's up, y'all? Where my mama at?"

"What's up, Mizzy Miz? What's good with you, baby sis?"

"Stop calling me that dumb shit, Melo."

"My bad, baby sis. Everything good with you?"

"I'm forever straight, you know me. What's going on, Kelsey? You not speaking today?"

"My fault, Mizzy, how are you today?"

"Hmm, I'm good. Where Mama at?"

"She in the kitchen with Mellissa. I heard what you said to her last night, so be nice, My'Zariah. Give her a chance."

The only time anyone ever called me My'Zariah was when they were serious and shit was important. I gave Melo the screw face because he knew how I felt about her, and for him to tell me to be nice was weird.

Deciding not to address what he just said, I walked off and headed to the kitchen to get this over with.

"Hey, Ma."

"There goes my baby. How are you today? Look at you, just glowing. So pretty."

"Thank you, Mama. Mellissa, how are you doing?

"I'm doing OK, My'Zariah. Thank you for asking."

The last thing I wanted to do was have a conversation with her, but I was raised to speak whenever I walked into a room. It didn't help that my grandmother was giving me the look she gave when she was tired of my bullshit.

"Now, Mizzy, I am going to get right to the reason I called you over here. Now I tried my best to raise you to be a very respectful child and woman, and for the most part, you have been and still are, but you have a mean streak just like your grandfather. Y'all don't share a birthday for nothing. Whenever y'all are faced with a situation where y'all feel uncomfortable, you lash out and that's what you did last night with Mellissa. Now, I can't tell you how to feel but I can tell you to be respectful. Despite everything, she is still your birth mother. I forgave my daughter a long time ago, and now, we think it's time you do the same."

This lady didn't waste any time getting to the point. She didn't even offer me a plate of what she had cooked, a glass of water or nothing, just straight on my case. Damn, I was kicking myself for not being high right now.

"Mama, with all due respect, I won't forgive her. What has she done for me where she should earn any respect from me, huh? Nothing but come in and out of my life whenever it was convenient for her. Not once has she called to wish me a happy birthday in twenty-one years, but now she wants to stay in town to spend time with me? Fuck all that. I am not wasting any of my time or energy on her. If that makes me the bad person, then so be it. I meant what I said last night and I'm not taking shit back."

"My'Zariah Michelle Preston, respect my house and watch your mouth. This ain't one of those bars you be going to where you can throw cuss words around like it's nothing. Watch your damn mouth in my house."

By this time, Mellissa was in the corner, wiping her tears with a napkin and sniffling, while Kelsey had her arm wrapped around her. She was putting on a show for everyone and they were all playing into her shit, but not me. In the words of Justin Timberlake, cry a river, for all I cared.

"Mizzy, I'm sorry. I am so sorry. I know it's hard but I need you to please try to forgive me."

"Why? Why should I?" I asked Mellissa as she sat there, still crying.

"Because I am your mother, and I want to have a relationship with you. I know you're grown now, but it's never too late."

"Let me stop you right there, Mellissa. You are not my mother, she is!" I yelled as I pointed to my grandmother. "That's the only mother I have, so try again. You want to clear your conscience for walking away from me, that's what it is."

"Mizzy, I'm sick. I didn't want to tell you like this but I have cancer. I am not trying to get any sympathy from you, but I needed you to know what was going on with me. That's why I am staying in Charlotte, for treatment. I wanted to spend some time with you in case the treatments don't work. I don't want to leave this earth with my only child hating me. To me, anything is better than nothing. Anytime with you is better than no time with you."

As if I could feel myself getting sick, I grabbed the corner and took a few deep breaths. The room was starting to spin and I felt that, at any moment, I would fall. Quickly, I grabbed one of the bar stools and took a seat. What the hell was going on around me? All of a sudden, they wanted to drop this shit on me. Mellissa saying she had cancer was the last thing I expected to hear today. It was like everything was crashing down on me at one time.

"Baby sis, you OK?" I saw Melo's lips moving, but I was so caught up, I honestly didn't hear what he said. From reading his lips, he was asking me if I was OK, and truthfully, I was not. I was starting to feel very closed in as everyone stared at me, waiting on me to say something, but what could I honestly say right now? For the first time in a while, I was speechless. After a few more minutes, I was able to open my eyes without the room feeling like it was closing in on me. Kelsey had grabbed a chair and moved it closer to Mellissa while Melo and my grandmother both sat on each side of me. They had their hands on my back, rubbing in an up and down motion. Melo and I had always been close, so just like Keon, I knew he always had my back. Now, Kelsey was a little different. Although we had a pretty good relationship, it was never as tight as me Melo and Ke and that was being shown even now as she sat next to Mellissa, consoling her.

"Mizzy, say something, please."

"What am I supposed to say, Mama? Y'all bring me here to tell me she has cancer, and y'all expect me to do what? Forgive her for twenty-one years of neglect? No, y'all got the wrong one.

"She over there crying like her life is ending tomorrow. Did she think about spending any time with me when she was so busy living her best life after I was born? Nah, she said fuck me and bounced. And you, Kelsey, over there

41

consoling her like she is sister of the year. Fuck outta here with all that fake ass love. Y'all can keep that shit."

"Mizzy, come on, sis, don't act like that. You know I have never been one to tell you no or tell you that you are wrong for how you felt because no one knows that but you. Mama and Mellissa are not asking you to spend all of your time with her, but you can at least try to understand where they're coming from."

"No, Melo, I can't and I won't. Mama, I am sorry for being disrespectful, but I'm not doing this. She does not get to choose when she wants to be a mother to me. Save the tears because they don't faze me. I gotta get out of here."

Right now, my emotions were everywhere, and before I disrespected my grandmother any further, I grabbed my things and walked out. Thank God for push to start because as soon as I got in, I sped off. My tires screeched as I rounded the corner, not even bothering to stop or slow down. I made it about half a mile from the house to a nearby park before the tears I tried so hard to hold back came out. I refused to give anyone the benefit of seeing me cry, but as I sat there all alone, I couldn't fight them anymore. I really needed Keon right now, but I didn't want to be selfish and ruin his date with Malik. I decided to call Ryan to see if he was still at my house. I really needed to talk to someone, since Ke was busy Ryan was my next choice.

"What's up, baby girl? How did it go at your grandparents's?"

"Everything is so fucked up, Ryan. Where are you? I just need to talk."

"I'm on the block right now, baby, but I won't be long."

"OK, just please don't make me wait all night."

"I got you baby girl."

Feeling defeated and irritated with the entire situation, I put my car back in drive and headed home. I didn't have any intentions of speaking to anyone, so I made sure my phone was on do not disturb.

Keon "Ke" Preston

Tonight, Malik and I were going to Ruth's Chris Steak House for our date night. I was so excited that he remembered how much I loved that restaurant. My man was really showing out for me. Hopefully, tonight would be the night he told me he was ready to tell his family about us.

My family really liked Malik, which was a plus in my book. Even when we would break up, my siblings always had good things to say about him. They never interfered in our relationship so they didn't know of any problems we had, and I wanted to keep it that way. I only felt comfortable giving bits and pieces to Mizzy. I knew she would never judge me, but being in my community, I always felt everyone wouldn't understand our paths and lifestyles.

I finally made it home and I had about three hours before our reservations. I wanted to take my time and pick the perfect outfit for the night. Checking my phone, I realized I had not heard back from Mizzy and I wanted to know how everything went at our parents's house. I loved my big sister Mellissa just as much as I loved Melo and Kelsey, but I didn't understand why she was so pressed to form this mother-daughter relationship with Mizzy. Everyone knew Mizzy wasn't with the shits when it came to her birth mother. She only saw my mother as her mother.

Sitting down on one of my barstools, I went to my contacts and tapped the FaceTime icon for Mizzy.

"Hello?"

"Bitch, why you got the camera off? I wanna see your ugly face. Don't tell me you got Ryan's dick in your mouth."

"No, I'm just not in the mood to be seen right now."

I heard the sniffling clearly through the phone, which immediately pissed me off because why was she crying. The conversation couldn't have gone that bad for her to be crying like that.

"Mizzy, don't try to lie to me. Why are you crying? What happened at Mama and Daddy's house today?"

"Nothing you need to worry yourself with, Keon. You gotta

get ready for your date tonight."

"My'Zariah, don't even try to play me like that. Now
what's going on? Do I need to go to the house and have a
conversation with Mellissa? I love my sister but I don't kiss
her ass like Kelsey does. I will put her where she needs to
be behind you."

"Keon, I'm good, Ryan is on his way home and he and I
will just chill for the night. I really don't want to talk about
it. Go have a good night and we will get together tomorrow
after class."

"Mizzy, are you sure? We can reschedule for tonight.
Malik will be mad for a day, but he already knows the
world stops when it comes to you."

"Ke, no, I am good. I swear. Go have fun and call me
tomorrow morning."

"Bitch, I am calling you when I get home, so you better
answer."

"I will. I love you."

"I love you more, baby sister."

Grabbing a shot glass from the bar, I poured myself a shot of Patrón to calm my nerves. I was going to respect Mizzy's wishes and let it go for the night, but I was getting in somebody's shit tomorrow about my baby sister. What people failed to realize was, Mizzy was more than my sister; she was my best friend. I didn't give a fuck how DNA saw it, she was not my niece. We were just alike in so many ways. Although I was the oldest, I looked up to her. She had this confidence about her that she just knew she was that girl. I hated when she was down and out. I made it my duty to pick my baby back up to the confident woman I knew she was.

Allowing myself a minute to allow the burning of the liquor to stop and taking a couple of deep breaths, I was ready to push all negative thoughts to the back and get ready to enjoy my man.

Looking through my closet, I had an idea what I wanted to wear. The goal was just to execute the look to perfection.

Two hours later, I was headed to the restaurant to meet up with Malik. For some reason, I was nervous. This was the first time in a while that he'd planned something for us.

Stepping out of my car, the cool breeze sent a chill through my body. The mustard-colored turtleneck was my only defense against the wind. The black polo slacks, along with my black Chelsea boots completed my outfit. Malik loved when I let my locs hang so that was what I decided to do with them.

Scanning the parking lot, I saw Malik's truck parked two spaces down from where I'd parked. I sent him a quick text, letting him know I was walking in. Ruth's Chris was a very popular restaurant, so I was not surprised that it was packed and had a crowded waiting area.

"Hi, welcome to Ruth's Chris, do you have a reservation?"

"Hi! Yes, I am meeting someone. I was told he was here. Malik Myers."

"Yes, right this way."

I followed the little petite hostess as she led me over to Malik, who was sitting at the table, drinking a glass of wine, and looking like a whole meal. Before pulling out my chair and having a seat, I asked the waitress to bring me a tequila sunrise. They had the best, in my opinion.

"Hey, baby, you look good." I complimented him as he stared at me with a slight smirk.

"Thanks, love, so do you." Malik looked so good dressed in a pair of Gucci slacks, a cream-colored V-neck sweater, and Gucci loafers. It always amazed me how an outfit so simple could look so good on him. My man wasn't big on fashion, but he knew what looked good on him.

"How did the photoshoot go today?"

"It went really well. The photographer asked me to work with them on a few more projects coming up. We are supposed to meet up with him in a few days to go over contracts."

"That's good, baby. I am proud of you."

"Thank you. So what is the special occasion tonight? You don't usually plan dates. Not that I am complaining, I'm just surprised."

"There is no occasion, we just haven't spent a lot of time together the past few weeks. With all these upcoming cases and now you with photoshoots, looks like we are going to be really busy."

"Yeah, it looks that way, but we can still make time for each other, Malik. We can't let our careers take up all of our time. You acting like we will go weeks without seeing each other."

"I'm not saying that, but we won't be together as much. I will be staying at my place a lot more because of work."

"Just say what it is, Malik. You wanna take a break. This is the same shit you always try to pull when you need a break. Let me guess, your people asking you about your sexuality again? Is that what it is? It's always an issue when they start giving you heat. Why can't you just be honest and keep it real with them and yourself? I am not going to keep being hidden because you're ashamed of who you are. That's not fair to me and this relationship."

"I am not ashamed of who I am, I'm just not ready to be open about it. You have to understand where I am coming from. This shit ain't easy, you should know that. I have a real career, so I have a lot at stake here."

"Oh OK, I see what this is. You don't think that what I do for a living is a real career? You don't want your paralegal and stuck up ass lawyer coworkers to know your boyfriend is a makeup artist. I'm an embarrassment to you?"

"Keon, I did not mean it that way. I respect you and what you do for a living. I would never think of you as an embarrassment. I'm just not ready for the world to know that part of my life yet."

For the first time, I doubted if Malik really loved me. Never had I ever felt so low about anything. I didn't think I felt this much pain when I first came out to my family. Malik knew firsthand how I felt when they called me an embarrassment, and here he was, feeling the same way. Right now, I didn't feel loved at all. Every emotion I felt growing up came rushing back. I needed to get away from this man. We had broken up before, but this time, I felt we were really over.

"Keon, talk to me, please. I can't take this silent treatment. Can we please have an adult conversation?"

By this time, the waitress had returned, ready to take our orders. I took a deep breath before standing to walk out of the restaurant. I didn't want to be around Malik any longer. Without another word, I gave Malik one last look before walking out of the restaurant. What hurt more than what was just said at the table was the fact that he didn't even try to stop me from leaving.

I made it to my car and just sat there, hoping he would come behind me, but after five minutes of nothing, I started my car and headed home. I had no idea what would become of our relationship, but right now, I was good on him and on men period.

My'Zariah "Mizzy" Preston

Here it was, eleven at night, and Ryan was just walking into my house. I was more hurt than I was mad. The fact that I begged him not to make me wait all day for him and he still made me wait was crazy to me. If I wasn't worth a couple of hours to him, then why was I with him?

Shit with Ryan hadn't always been this toxic. I met Ryan at a party a few of my college friends were having. I was very anti-social but my roommate at the time begged me to go with her to this party. Against my better judgment, I went with her. The party was a vibe and the music was hitting. After a few drinks, I started to mellow out and interact with some of my classmates, until a group of boys walked through. They were all sexy, but the one with the locs stood out to me. To say he was fine would be keeping it simple. This boy was gorgeous from the milk chocolate skin that was covered in tattoos, the deep dimples that showed from every movement of his lips, and the diamond tooth gems that shined when he smiled. The way he chewed that gum had me wishing he would chew on me the same way.

I wasn't trying to make the first move but I knew he felt my eyes staring a hole through him. After what seemed like forever of me just looking at this man, he finally decided to come over to where I was.

"What's up, beautiful? Where ya man at?"

"I don't have a man."

"Ain't no way you this fine and single. You got a nigga somewhere."

"I have no reason to lie. I'm as single as a dollar bill."

"What's your name, beautiful?"

"My'Zariah, but you can call me Mizzy."

"Aight, Mizzy. I'm Ryan. Put my number in your phone and save me as your future."

"My future? You reaching a little bit, aren't you?"

"Nah, I go for what I want. No beating around the bush, baby."

It took a week before he even texted me, which should have been a red flag, but curiosity got the best of me and I wanted to test the waters and see just what Ryan was all about. The first six months for us were amazing. He did everything a boyfriend was supposed to do. Keon always told me I fell too fast but I didn't think so. Ryan was my first true love and, in my eyes, he could do no wrong. But, like most street niggas, his true colors started to show. I was too in love to see it.

Ryan got too comfortable, and I allowed it. I overlooked the shit he was doing. I honestly wanted to believe he was just constantly working, but I was dumb to what he was doing. I didn't have clear evidence that Ryan was cheating on me but his actions showed otherwise. I would never flat out go to him with any accusations but I was clearly going to ask some questions and see for myself how many lies he would tell.

The sound of my alarm going off interrupted my thoughts as I watched Ryan put in the code for the alarm, which so happened to be his birthday. I was definitely changing that code in the morning.

"What's wrong with you? Why you sitting in the dark?"

"Where you been, Ryan? And don't insult my intelligence and say working. Just be real with me. Where you been? Or should I ask, who have you been with?"

"Mizzy, you know what I do out here in these streets, why you trippin'? You act like I am not out here hustlin' and shit."

"Fuck that. I asked you—nah, fucking begged you—not to make me wait all day, and you couldn't give me that. I'm not good enough for a couple hours of your time when I needed you the most? Is that what you saying?

"So the question is, if I'm not getting any of your time, then who is? Hell, if it was that important, I could have given you the money you claim you would have been missing for a little bit of your time."

"Stop playing with me, girl. I done told you I am not fucking with nobody but you. What I look like, taking money from you when I'm your man? I apologize for not coming through earlier. I lost track of time. I'm here now, so talk, baby girl. What's going on?"

"I'm good on you. Your time is no longer needed, so whatever you were doing or whoever you were doing it with, you can go back. I promise you there are no hard feelings anymore 'cause I am done."

I knew I was too calm for my own good. The more I sat there and argued, the more my anger progressed. I wasn't a violent person but there was only so much a bitch could take. I was holding on by a thread and was threatening to lose it any minute.

I needed a hot shower just to wash away the stress of the day. I grabbed what I needed and headed for my bathroom. I turned on the water, setting it to the hottest temperature I could stand, and stepped in, letting the water run down my face and down my body. As much as I tried not to, I silently cried as my tears mixed with the hot water from the shower. I cried for my relationship with Ryan and I cried for my birth mother. As angry as I was for her leaving me, I never imagined her not being here physically.

The entire day, I questioned God why it took an illness for her to want to have any type of relationship with me. In my eyes, I was just a mistake to her. My liquid pain fell from my eyes as I felt the cool air on my body as the shower door opened. I looked over at Ryan as he stared at me. I was pissed that he was looking at me as I cried. The last thing I wanted was for him to see me as weak.

"Why you crying, ma? Look, I told you I was sorry for not coming to you earlier. What can I do to show you how sorry I am?"

"The only change I need is changed behavior. You been giving me false promises for a while now; I can't take it anymore, Ryan. I'm done with all of this and with you. I don't have any concrete evidence that you are fucking somebody else but your actions for the last few months have really made me question you and our relationship. I can't do this with you anymore, Ryan. Everything is coming at me at one time and I asked you to just be there for me and you couldn't. That's not showing me you love me. That's you giving me your ass to kiss. I'm done, Ryan, just leave."

"You done with me, Mizzy? You mean that? You really want me to go in there, pack my shit, and leave? Is that what you're saying? Look me in my eyes and tell me you are done with me and want me out of your life. Say it."

I watched as Ryan removed the black rubber band from his wrist and placed his locs in a bun on the top of his head. Next, he removed the black t-shirt he was wearing and tossed it on the floor, followed by his baller shorts and Polo boxers. Of course, my pussy betrayed me and I was dripping, looking at this man standing in front of me naked. The words he was speaking fell on deaf ears. I was in another world, lusting over this man. I couldn't find my voice. I knew what I wanted to say, but I couldn't find the words; they were stuck. I was stuck.

I used my finger to trace the serpent tattoo that flowed across his chest, down to the tattoo that spelled out the word loyalty across his stomach. Ryan was an outie and I loved playing with his navel, so I took a minute to trace one of my favorite body parts on him. My tears were mixed with the warm water flowing down my face. By now, Ryan had invaded my personal space and was standing in front of me as the water dripped down his back. This man was covered in tattoos and I loved every one of them.

"I'm waiting, Mizzy. Tell me we are done and I will leave right now. I'll give you what you're asking for, just say the words."

57

I knew what I wanted to say, but my words were stuck. I was mute and in a state of lust. Ryan was blessed with eyes that drew you in to him. I closed my eyes as Ryan's soft lips grazed across mine. He teased me as his hands roamed up and down my sides.

"You want me to stop?"

"No," I whispered as he used his finger to play with my clit. My knees started to feel weak so I wrapped both arms around his neck to keep from falling. Our lips met and I allowed him to slip his tongue in my mouth. The chewing gum mixed with weed was intoxicating. I felt my release building up just from the way he gently toyed with my clit.

"Let that shit out, Mizzy. All on my hand, baby."

"Ryan!" My voice was shaky and my words were slurring as I came so hard. The harder my body shook, the faster Ryan played with my clit, driving me over the edge. Two nuts back to back and I was drained, but I knew Ryan wasn't done with me.

"Turn around and put your hands on the wall." The deep

baritone voice held so much authority, I did as he asked and waited for whatever pleasure he was about to put my body through.

I jumped as I felt Ryan's tongue slide across my pussy. I spread my legs a little more to allow him access to go deeper.

"You taste good, ma. This shit so sweet." Ryan licked on me like I was his favorite lollipop and I was enjoying it. I was close to another climax when I felt all nine inches of his dick enter me. He wasn't super hung but he had a curve that was dangerous.

"Fuck, Ryan… Shit!"

"Throw that ass back, ma. Give me that pussy. Damn, you gripping the fuck out of my dick, ma."

"I'm cummin'… Ooooohhhh fuck!"

"Fuck, this pussy feels so good. You better not ever try to leave, girl. This pussy too good. Damn, I love this shit. You gon' leave me, Mizzy? I swear I'm not fucking nobody but you, baby. You gotta believe me. I love the shit out of you, ma."

"Ryan, baby, don't stop pleaseeeeeee."

"I love you, ma. I promise we gon' get back right. Do you trust me?"

"Yes!"

"Good girl. Do you love me?"

"Yes, I love you, Ryan."

"That's my girl. Cum one more time for me, baby. I'm almost there."

After a few more minutes of slow fucking, we came together. Thankfully, I took my birth control faithfully because this nigga shot all in me. He had a weak ass pull-out game.

After I came down from my high, I was kicking myself for not standing my ground with Ryan. I was so prepared to end things with him but I was caught in a moment of weakness and he took advantage of that. I love Ryan, but I was no longer in love with him. Once again, I allowed this man to get in my head.

"Fuck," I said to myself as I stood under the water, allowing more tears to flow. I had to be strong when we talked in the morning.

Ryan Marshall

Looking over at Mizzy as she slept so peacefully, I didn't want to wake her, but we needed to have a talk. I kept hearing her tell me it was over between us and that was never happening. I needed her to know she was locked in with this death row contract for life.

Mizzy had something no other bitch had and that was my heart. I fucked with a lot of hoes but none of them held me down like she did. We hit a rough patch, I could admit that, but my heart was in her hands and I was locked in. Her telling me what she told me last night had a nigga shook. I needed to get my shit together and get back right with my shorty. I couldn't let her dip out on me.

I was wrong as fuck for not being there for her like she needed me to and I was going to make up for that. Truth was, I was with a bitch I fucked with from time to time and I lost track of time. She wasn't just a bitch I let suck my dick sometimes; she was a street bitch and I trusted her with my product and my money.

After spending so much time with the bitch, we started fucking around. I would never stash shit at Mizzy's place because I didn't want her to ever be caught up in the drug game. My shorty wasn't in the streets like that and I needed her to stay that way. I didn't plan on doing this shit for long. My end goal was to open my barbershop and turn this money legal. After that, I was marrying Mizzy, so I just needed her to bear with me for a little while longer. I was cutting all these bitches off when the time came.

"Mizzy, wake up, ma. We need to talk." Even with that smirk on her face, my shorty was the baddest bitch in Queen City. Her loyalty to a nigga made me fall hard for her.

The night I met her at the party and had her save me as her future, I was speaking that shit into existence. I needed her to know I was the one that was going to make her happy. Our shit ain't no fairytale relationship, but I promised her when we made shit official, I would be the man she dreamed about, and I stood on that shit.

"My'Zariah, get up, baby. I am taking you out so we can talk."

"What do you need to talk about, Ryan? Whatever you gotta say, you can do it here. I'm not going anywhere with you."

"Mizzy, look, I am sorry. I can't say that shit enough. You told me you needed changed behavior and I am going to give you that, but you trying to break up with me ain't happening."

"You can't make me stay with you, Ryan. I am tired of the disrespect. Fucking you last night was a mistake. You don't respect me, you don't spend no time with me, so what are we doing here, Ryan? I needed you yesterday and you brushed me off like I was nothing. How am I supposed to feel about that, Ryan?"

"Baby, I am so sorry. I lost track of time yesterday. You know I am trying to get my shop open and turn this money legal, but until that happens, I gotta be in these streets, ma."

"I am tired of hearing I am sorry. I heard that shit so much yesterday until I am numb to the word sorry. Apologies don't mean shit to me unless it comes with changes. Ryan, I love you. I love you to the point I was overlooking the shit you were doing. Not coming home, coming home late, not answering my calls, all that. I'm not putting up with this shit no more. It's plenty of niggas out there who would treat me better."

"Stop playing with me, girl. Ain't no other nigga out there because I'm not letting another nigga think he has a chance. What we got is for life, Mizzy."

64

"For life? You sound crazy as fuck right now."

"How you just gon' throw away what we have, Mizzy? Shit ain't perfect, but no relationship is. Everybody goes through shit, ma. You can't just give up."

"Ryan, please miss me with that Cosby Show shit. You ain't Cliff and I ain't Claire, so please cut that shit out. We have not been good for a while and you know it. You been moving funny for months. I was just letting shit fly by because I do love you, but I am tired, Ryan."

"Baby, listen to me, OK? I'm not doing anything but trying to make this money for us. I'm gon' marry you one day soon, and we gon' toss them birth control pills 'cause I want you to give me some babies. We gon' be straight. I promise you we are. Just don't leave me, please. I ain't even with all this toxic shit and you know that."

I knew my shorty, and I was breaking her down. I wasn't trying to make her cry but I needed her to understand that I was fighting for what was mine and My'Zariah was mine. Not in a possessive kind of way, but my girl was my fucking future.

"Mizzy, look at me. I need you to understand that I am not playing when it comes to you and me. We got something special, ma. Something nobody can break."

"Ryan, I swear to God if you make me regret my decision to give you another chance, I will kill you. Don't make me regret this."

"Come here, girl, with your mean ass. You not killing nobody, girl. You know I love you, right? This shit is forever. Till death, baby."

It took a lot of begging and convincing, but I finally got Mizzy to listen to me and understand that nothing was coming between us. I wasn't a nigga who was afraid to beg. Niggas might clown me but I begged for my shorty.

After a few more minutes of kissing up to my girl, I needed to head out and make some money. I also needed to head to this bitch's house to re-up on my product. I hoped her ass wasn't on bullshit and trying to fuck because I wasn't in the mood and I didn't want to fuck and risk shit with Mizzy. I had to make sure Mizzy was good before I headed out.

Pulling up to Azela's house, I parked, walked up and let myself in. I'd been fucking with Azlea long before Mizzy and I got together. She was a runner for a few of the niggas on the block, so she knew the ins and outs of our operations. She was hood as fuck but also smart. The bitch was a diamond in the rough for sure. She could be loyal to all the niggas in the hood but couldn't be faithful to a nigga who was trying to wife her ass. The bitch was fucking with more niggas than a damn stripper taking advantage in the private room.

"What's good, baby daddy?"

"Stop playing with me, you know that baby ain't mine. He could belong to any nigga on the block, so stop trying to pin that shit on me. I strap up every time and pull out, shorty, so try again."

"Yet you scared to take a DNA test."

"I ain't scared of shit. I know the lil nigga ain't mine, unless you poked holes in the condom and I know you ain't that dumb. Ain't no way he mine. Go test one of the niggas you be fucking with."

"We didn't use protection every time, Ryan. Plus, you keep coming back for more, so something got you hooked."

"I am not about to go back and forth with you this morning. Go get my bag and shit so I can re-up and head out."

"You don't have to rush out, Ryan. I cooked, you hungry?"

"Yeah, you can fix me something and make sure ain't no pork on my plate."

"I know you don't eat pork. I have turkey sausage and turkey bacon for you."

I didn't realize how hungry I was until Azalea said something. I wanted to take Mizzy out for a little breakfast date but I had to spend most of the morning, getting back into her good graces. I wanted to plan something special for my shorty and I was doing that very soon. Maybe a little getaway for us or something.

I really didn't plan to be here too long, but I couldn't front, that food smelled good as fuck, and my stomach was grumbling something serious.

"Here you go. What do you want to drink?"

"Let me get a bottle of water."

"Here. How long you staying?"

"Not long, I got plans tonight."

"Plans doing what, and with who?"

"The fuck is with all these questions? What is this, an interrogation? You wired or some shit?"

"No, I'm not wired. I just wanted to know if you was gon' spend some time with me."

"Nah, like I told you, I got plans. And how you trying to spend time with me? Where your baby at? You stay trying to pin that lil nigga on somebody but you never have him."

"He is with my mama. I don't like him being around all these drugs and shit and niggas popping up whenever they feel like it. Plus, she keeps him while I work."

"You must work twenty-four seven 'cause he ain't never here. You need to stop playing and find out who his daddy is and stop just assuming."

"I ain't gotta assume shit. I know who his daddy is, and if you stop being so scared and take the test, you would know, too. But since you so sure you not the daddy, just take the test and prove me wrong."

"Bitch, I'm not about to take no DNA test on a baby I know I didn't father. You outta your goddamn mind."

"Yeah, all right, Ryan. I think you gotta feeling he could be yours, but you can keep playing dumb with me."

"And what makes you so sure he mine, anyway? Do you know how many boys on the block claim they fucked you?"

"Well, they can claim all they want, but I ain't fuck with all them niggas. Niggas lie on they dick all the time. Half them motherfuckers ain't never stepped foot in my house; I meet them at the door."

"Yeah, OK. Fool somebody else with that lie."

"Why you assume I'm lying, Ryan? Just prove me wrong."

"Look, lil mama, I appreciate what you do for me by stashing my shit and holding a nigga down, but what we got is coming to an end real soon. I'm about to wife my shorty and I don't need no outside interference or drama, and you hood as fuck, so drama follows you."

"Wife who? Nigga, you ain't about to make nobody your wife. That bitch would be a fool to marry you. When have you ever been faithful? Hell, we been fucking since ninth grade and you ain't never been faithful. You always come back to me."

"Well, you ain't gotta worry about me coming back, lil mama. Not to fuck, that is."

This bitch was starting to annoy me with all these damn questions. Had me thinking she was about to set my ass up. It was time to start making moves to distance myself from her, but right now, I needed to be smart about my plans.

"Thanks for the food and everything, I'll be back in a few days. Hold it down, ma."

"That's it? You just gon' eat and run? You can't stay for a

little while longer?"

As she got closer to me, I saw her pussy through the little ass shorts she had on. I couldn't lie, my dick got hard looking at her. Any man with twenty-twenty vision could see she was beautiful in that exotic way. I didn't know how many inches her weave was but that shit hung down past her ass cheeks and it was a deep ass red. Her ass was fat and wiggled with every step she took. The way she was staring at my dick had a nigga contemplating if I wanted to let her give me some head.

"You know you want me, Ryan. Why you trying to run? You ain't married yet, so you still single in my eyes."

"Nah, you right. I'm not married yet, but I'm good, sweetheart."

That shit took will power but my mind was on the bigger picture, which was my money and my shorty. I couldn't let irrelevant shit distract me from my main goal. Shit, I could get pussy at home with my shorty, so there was no need for a side bitch. I was done with all that shit. Shit was hitting too close to home and I almost lost my shorty for my fuck ups. I needed to make some changes to keep Mizzy happy. I just hoped Azalea played her part and didn't start no shit, especially with her trying to pin her baby on me.

It was also time for me to have a conversation with my plug about switching shit up. I needed to get someone in position to take my spot when I gave all this up. Shit was getting too close to home in more ways than one.

Jadarius (JD) White

"Where is this nigga at with my money? He better not be fucking with that bitch Azela and wasting my time. My time is valuable." I sat parked at one of my stash houses, waiting on this nigga Ryan to pull up with my money. For the most part, the nigga was cool and I never had any issues but the nigga had no respect for time.

I told all my workers, if you're early, you're on time, if you're on time, you're late. That's how I ran all my businesses and that shit made me successful. With all of my businesses, I didn't really have time to be here like a sitting duck, waiting."

"Call that nigga up and see how long he gon' have me waiting," I said to my brother, Johntae, who was sitting on the driver's side.

"What you in such a rush for? You must got some pussy waiting on you or something, the way you carrying on."

"Don't worry about what I got waiting on me, nigga, just call that man up so I can head out."

I heard the conversation Johntae was having with Ryan, and just as I expected, he was leaving Azela's crib. The man was so busy playing house with that bitch, he was wasting my time. Nothing pissed me off more than a nigga letting pussy come before money, especially from a bitch who belonged to the streets. That was exactly why I was single and planned on being single for a long ass time. Bitches came with too much baggage and that could lead to a lot of unnecessary shit I didn't need.

Don't get shit twisted, I got pussy, and plenty of it, but I wasn't no pillow-talking motherfucker. I never took a bitch to my crib, and I never led them on to think that it was more than just a fuck. Yeah, there was a few I doubled back with because their pussy was good, but never no feelings. Most females developed feelings too fast; I didn't have time for that shit. The only thing that made my dick hard more than pussy was money.

"That nigga on the way, but for real, what you in such a hurry for? You live alone and ain't no bitch waiting at the crib for you. Come to the club with us. Shit, you might find you a freak to take home."

"Nah, I'm cool on the club. I got a few business meetings

tomorrow, and the rest of the week, so I will be unavailable for a few days. I'll need you and Ryan to keep shit moving."

"You already know I got you, big brother. You ain't got to worry about nothing."

"Yeah, I know. You're going to be in charge of all of this soon, so here is your chance to prove you are ready."

"You know I am ready, nigga. I have been itching to take over this shit since I was sixteen. You and Pops did y'all big one by training me, so I am ready."

"You gotta be focused, Tae. You can't let nothing take your attention away from the money. I know you a young nigga and females got your attention, but don't let pussy kill your focus and get you killed or locked up, you hear me?"

"Yeah, I hear you, JD. I know what I am doing. You kept me under your wing for so long, I have learned everything I need to know from you. You can trust me."

"I know I can, but I gotta tell you, Tae. I don't need nothing to happen to you."

"Aight, I feel you. There go that nigga Ryan right there."

"'Bout fucking time."

Getting out of the car, I made sure to check my
surroundings at the same time, making sure my gun was on
my waist. You could never be too careful around here.
There would always be a little nigga that grew balls and
thought they could take over the streets. I was always
taught to be one step ahead of everything.

"My fault, JD. I didn't mean to have you waiting so long.
Me and my girl got into it last night and this morning, so
my mind was somewhere else, and Azalea on that bullshit
again about that baby being mine. I know for a fact that
baby ain't mine. I strapped up every time I hit it."

Standing back, listening to Ryan complain about his girl,
was just the shit I was telling Johntae. Here this nigga was,
talking about him and his girl getting into it, but could
possibly have a baby from another bitch. This motherfucker
had a lot of growing up to do if you asked me. He allowed
the wrong shit to cloud his judgment. The shit wasn't a
good look at all and was bad for business.

"Let me ask you something, Ryan. How do you plan to run your business with you juggling two women? That's unnecessary drama you could potentially bring to my operation. That's not a good look and I don't need no female drama causing you to fuck up and lose focus."

"It ain't even that deep, JD. Azelea is just in her feelings because she can't pin that baby on me and I'm not fucking with her no more."

"Why you fucking with her in the first place, nigga? That bitch probably fuck with half of the city, man. If you got a girl, why you fucking with a hoe like that? And raw, my nigga."

"Look, JD, I don't mean no disrespect, but what I got going on is really none of anyone's concern. I do my job, my money count ain't never short, and my product always sells out. I don't let shit stop me from doing what I need to do, so I don't need a lecture from anybody. Now, you got my word that nothing will stop me from continuing to do what I do until I can get my shit right."

"Yeah, I hear you , but I see otherwise. You just better hope this shit don't backfire on your ass."

"Ain't shit gon' backfire, trust me."

After that, I dropped the conversation and finished my count. The last thing I wanted to do was lecture a grown ass man on who he was fucking. As long as his drama didn't interfere with my money, I was cool on him. My main focus was these upcoming meetings I had. I was ready to expand my realty company across a few more states. I already had businesses in the Carolinas and Georgia. I wanted the entire southeast, and hopefully, the Midwest.

Real estate had been a passion of mine since I was young. Owning multiple properties that I could turn into any business I wanted was the ultimate goal. Right now, I had three strip clubs in both North and South Carolina, two apartment complexes in both states and Georgia and was currently working on a strip mall in Georgia. After these meetings, I would hopefully own some land to build a brand new apartment complex. I was pushing twenty-five and ready to get out of the drug game. Most niggas did this shit for the long haul, but not me, which was why I decided to go to college after high school for business. I ran a smooth operation while pursuing a bachelor's degree and eventually my masters, while still running this drug operation. The streets and the hustle had always been in my blood. I was raised around this shit from birth. From my grandfather to my father and uncles and now me and my little brother.

I always said I didn't want to do this shit past thirty, but truth was, I was and would always be a street nigga. I just knew when it was time to step down and let the next man take over while I watched from my own throne.

Keon "Ke" Preston

For the first time in a long time, I laid in my bed, contemplating life and my life choices. I knew when I came out that my life would forever be changed and I would be looked at differently by many people, family included, but after what was told to me last night, I was back in that dark space. I worked so hard to get out of that space, prayed to never get back there, but what Malik told me hurt me to my core. For him to tell me he was basically embarrassed about what I choose to do with my life really stung me.

I had been doing makeup for as long as I could remember, even before I came out to my family. I remember late nights, me and Mizzy would stay up and watch makeup videos and I would use her as my model. I was so in love with the transformation makeup had on women, especially Black women. Black women were already beautiful in their natural state, but adding a little makeup took that beauty to a whole other level and I wanted to be a part of that.

81

Right now, I felt like I'd made a mistake with the road I chose for myself. I looked over at my phone at yet another missed call from Malik. The best thing for me to do was to block him but I just couldn't do that. Deep down, I wanted him to call me and apologize for the way he made me feel, but I didn't want to answer for him when he called. I was confused, hurt, and angry all at once. I wanted to call Mizzy but I didn't want to drag her in my relationship drama yet again. I didn't know what the future held for Malik and I but I couldn't keep getting put into this dark space.

The ringing of my phone pulled me away from my thoughts and I saw Mizzy's picture pop up on my phone. I didn't want to answer but that was not how Mizzy and I did things. We never hid anything from one another, so now was the best time to tell her what was going on.

"Hello?"

"Come open the door, I got Starbucks."

Damn, this bitch must be going through some shit, too. That's the only time she ever drank Starbucks. Before I could say anything, the phone went dead and I realized she had hung up on me.

Slinging my cover to the other side of my bed, I got up to let my sister in. Opening the door, one look at Mizzy and I could tell she had been crying. She looked exhausted.

"I fucked up, Keon. Really fucked up. Everything is messed up right now."

"Why you look like you been crying? When I called you yesterday, you were crying. What's going on, sis?"

"I don't even know where to start. Well, apparently, your sister is staying in Charlotte because she has cancer. I was ready to be done with Ryan, but of course, I let him fuck with my head last night. I'm just so confused."

"Wait, back up. Mellissa has cancer? How? What kind of cancer? What stage? How is she doing?"

"I don't know all of that. I didn't stay long enough to ask any questions. She started crying and acting a fool, apologizing and shit. She was putting on a show and Kelsey was eating it up, so I just left. I wasn't about to sit there and fake like I felt sorry for her, 'cause honestly, I don't and that's so fucked up of me, Ke. I don't feel sympathy for my birth mother, who was just diagnosed with cancer. What type of person am I?"

"This is too much, and Kelsey, with her big back, messy ass gotta do the most. I just know my mama is having a hard time accepting this. Lord have mercy."

"Mama was so focused on me forgiving Mellissa, honestly, so I don't know how she is taking this."

"So, what they want you to do? Go to the doctor with her and shit? I just don't understand all this."

"Me either, but here is where the shit gets fucked up. When I left the house, I didn't want to call and bother you because I knew you were doing the photoshoot and had your date with Malik, so I called Ryan and asked him to come home because I needed someone to talk to and listen to me. You know this pigeon toed motherfucker had the nerve to walk in my house at eleven at night, after I begged him not to make me wait. He had me waiting for him like I'm some dope fiend on the damn street. What type of shit is that? Then he walked in the house like he ain't did shit wrong. I'm over all this shit."

"Niggas ain't shit, I tell you that much. I am done with Malik for good this time."

"You always say that and be right back with him. In a few days, you will be singing, my man, my man, my man. You are not serious."

"No, Mizzy, this time, I am serious. I am tired of him not being honest with his people about us. I feel like he is hiding me, and last night, he basically told me I was an embarrassment to him because of the career path I chose."

"That no neck fucker. I know you lying. Did he really say that to you?"

"Not in so many words, but in those words."

I held back tears as I told her what all went down last night at the restaurant. The more I talked about it, the worse I felt. I was starting to feel like my love life and life in general was just one big disappointment. Out of everyone in my life, the only person who truly understood me was Mizzy, and she was going through her own issues right now. I needed to be strong for her, but right now, I was showing weakness. Everyone thought Mizzy was so mean and hardcore, but deep down, she was hurting but she would never show it. She was so used to being so hardcore that she refused to show weakness, but right now, she was breaking.

"Keon, I am so sorry you had to go through that. I can't and won't tell you what to do, but fuck him. He does not deserve you. How can he say you don't have a real career? Stupid bastard."

"Yeah, I know. Is it dumb of me to want him to apologize to me? That's stupid, right?"

"It's not dumb at all because he honestly owes you an apology and an explanation for why he would feel that way. What would make him come at you like that? Sounds like he is embarrassed about himself."

"I don't think it's as much of him being embarrassed, but more so of what his family would say."

"I get it, honestly, I do, Keon, but that storyline is getting played out. People need to come to terms with themselves and say fuck what anyone else has to say. Look at me. People are going to say I should forgive Mellissa but I'm not because she doesn't deserve my forgiveness."

"You're right, sis. So what's up with Ryan? I know you cussed his dog ass out last night."

"No, I didn't have any words for his ass, but what pissed me off is him coming into my shower and seeing me cry. I hate to seem weak to anyone, and last night, he saw me at my lowest and used my moment of weakness to his advantage."

"Took advantage of you how?"

"How do you think? He fucked me to sleep. I told him I didn't want to be with him anymore and he wasn't taking that. I told him if he made me regret my decision to give him a second chance, I would kill him."

"That dick will do it every time, bitch!"

"But I don't want to do this with him no more. I really don't want to. I just think I should be single forever."

"I guess we can be single together, sis, 'cause I can't deal with no more heartache from nobody."

"Fuck it, let's just pack up and leave on our getaway. We can book a cabin or whatever while we drive. I don't want to fly or be in a crowded ass airport. I just need to get away from everything."

"OK, Mizzy, we can do that, but I need to meet with Zakari first to see when he needs me for his next photoshoot. He asked me to work with him again and I said I would. You can go pack while I text him to see if we can meet up real quick."

"That sounds like a plan. I need this, Keon, thank you."

"Bitch, don't thank me. We both need this shit."

Mizzy and I sat around, talking about our plans for another hour before she decided to go ahead and head out. I would never tell her what to do, but I felt she needed to have a conversation with Mellissa to get out all of her emotions. I knew it was a long shot but it needed to be done.

After seeing Mizzy off, I grabbed my phone and sent Zakari a text, asking him if we could meet at a local coffee shop not too far from the first photoshoot location. Thankfully, he wasn't busy and was able to meet me.

I really didn't want to put much effort into getting dressed, but I learned a long time ago to never leave your house without putting in a little effort. So, I threw on a pair of Adidas track pants, a basic black tee and black Yeezy slides, and headed out to meet up with Zakari. For some reason, I was extremely nervous. Maybe because there was an attraction there, but nothing serious, especially with me. I needed to focus on me and my relationship with Malik, or lack thereof, I should say.

About twenty minutes later, I was pulling up to the coffee shop. I spotted Zakari sitting outside of the shop at one of the tables. I sent a quick text, letting him know I was here and parking. The attraction I felt when I walked out to the sitting area and our eyes locked was like something out of a movie. The way he licked his lips when he looked up at me made me happy I'd put in some effort to look somewhat decent today.

"Glad you could make it on such short notice."

"Yeah, no problem. Have a seat and order whatever you'd like. My treat."

"I'll just take a bottle of water."

I waited as Zakari called over the waitress and ordered my water, along with another coffee for himself. Just like the last time I saw him, he was dressed casually in a pair of black biker jeans, a purple Lakers jersey and a pair of purple and black Dunks. This was one good-looking man.

"Let me keep it real with you, Keon. I have a lot of photo shoots coming up for some major companies and I need a full-time makeup artist. After your work with the last shoot, I want you on my team. You really had my girls looking beautiful. I didn't have to do as much editing as I had to do previously. You matched their skin tones perfectly and they looked so natural. I have the contracts now and we can discuss payments. The next shoot will be in two weeks. So, will you do me the honor and join my team?"

"I honestly don't know what to say. I am flattered that you think my work is good enough to be exclusive to you and your team. I would love to join and work with you."

"Awesome, Keon. Welcome aboard and thank you for taking my offer. I have the contracts for you to sign. You can take them with you and go over them."

Zakari passed the folder containing the contracts over to me and there was an instant spark when our hands touched. The shit scared me to be truthful. I had never felt a spark so intense before. I slowly pulled my hand back and pulled the folder close to me. I didn't want to seem rude and pull out the contracts and just start reading them in front of him. My plan was to take them with me to Tennessee so I could have Mizzy go over them with me.

"Again, I can't thank you enough for this opportunity. You really helped turn my day around. I appreciate you."

"I'm glad I can help make your day a little brighter. How about I make your night? Let me take you out to dinner tonight?"

Damn, was this man coming on to me? Here I was, suffering from a heartbreak, and my soon-to-be new work partner was asking me on a date. Even if I wasn't preparing to leave on vacation, I didn't think I would go out with him. Hell, I didn't know if I was single or not, so going out with someone right now would be too much.

"So, Keon, what do you say? Can I treat you to dinner and welcome you to the team?"

"Zakari, I would love to have dinner with you tonight, but when I finish up here, My'Zariah and I are driving to Tennessee on a little mini vacation for a few days."

"OK, that's fine, but when you get back, hit me up. We can make plans then."

The way he looked at me had my palms sweating and my heart racing. What the hell was going on? Was he really flirting with me? I wasn't too sure if working with him was a good idea if there would be this much attraction, but this was the opportunity I needed to really get my foot in the door in this industry. I needed to suck it up and do it.

"I will let you know when I get back in town and I will have the contracts signed."

"I see you trying to dodge my offer to take you out to dinner."

"I'm not dodging it, I'm just dealing with a situation right now and I don't want there to be any confusion."

"I can respect that and your situation, but if you change your mind when you come back, you got the number. Use it."

"I will let you know when I get back in town so I can give you the contracts."

No matter how hard I tried to hide the smile on my face, I couldn't hide it. I found it cute the way he flirted with me. It was like a schoolboy crush. If I wasn't dealing with this shit with Malik, I would not hesitate to take him up on his offer. Right now was just not it.

I finished my water and grabbed my keys to go.

"I'm gonna get up out of here so we can hit the road. I will make sure to use your number when I get back."

"Cool. Y'all drive safe and have a good time. And whatever your situation-ship is, don't let it ruin your vacation."

"Thank you, Zakari. I appreciate you." With that, I walked away, back to my car, adding an extra switch in my walk, knowing he would be watching extra hard. I had to mentally prepare myself to work with him, knowing there was a deep attraction coming from both of us. Even if me and Malik never got back together, I was good on any new relationship for a long time.

My'Zariah "Mizzy" Preston

After the last few days I'd had, I was finally happy to be getting out of Charlotte for a few days. I was leaving the drama that was my life and hopefully coming back with a clear mind, ready to take on the shitshow I had been dealt. At almost twenty-two years of life, this was the first time I had really felt confused and weak. I had always been so strong, but knowing that the woman who gave birth to me and then abandoned me could be dying. A part of me questioned if she was lying to get sympathy out of me, but then why would she put my grandmother through something like that? Maybe deep down, I was hoping she was lying. The shit was just crazy to me. I was ready to put all this shit behind me for a few days.

Pulling my Steve Madden luggage set out of my closet, I started to pack everything I would need for a few days. Fall was still in the air, so I decided to pack a few of my sweat suits I'd just recently purchased. Also, a few pieces to choose from for dinner and the clubs we liked to go to when we visited. In the middle of me packing, I heard my front door open. Out of all days, this man decided to come home early today. I wanted to pack and go back to Keon's house until we left and send him a text that I was going on vacation for a few days. I knew that would have been petty of me but I didn't want to see him until I was able to sort out my feelings.

"What are you doing, ma?"

"Packing, what does it look like?"

"I see you packing, but why? Where you going? I thought we talked about this? Why you trying to leave me?"

"I'm not leaving you, dummy. Keon and I are going on a little vacation for a few days. I just need to get out of North Carolina for a bit, so chill."

"When did you plan on telling me?"

"Honestly, when we were halfway to our destination."

"You say that shit like you right. You were just going to

95

leave and not say shit? That's the petty shit you on now, My'Zariah?"

"Please calm the fuck down, Ryan. I wasn't being petty. I was going to tell you, just when I felt like it. It's not like I'm going to stay and not come back. I said a few days."

"That's not the point though, ma. We supposed to be getting us back on track. Just last night, you was talking about we were done and shit, and now you going on vacation with your brother. Why didn't you plan a vacation for us?"

"Are you serious? You can't even come home at a decent hour at night, but you wanna go on vacation? Get the fuck outta here, Ryan. Keon and I have been planning this for a while, so don't act like that."

"So where y'all going?"

"Why?"

"You can't tell me where you going? What type of shit is that?"

"What you want to know for? Damn, Ryan, you being real fucking aggressive right now. I'm leaving North Carolina, that's all you need to know."

"Why you being so secretive all of a sudden, Mizzy? We used to tell each other everything, now you keeping secrets and leaving town and not telling me. What changed with you, ma?"

"You should be asking yourself that, Ryan. You're the one that has changed. Look, I don't have time to stand here and argue back and forth with you on a relationship that's fucked up at the moment. Now, if you don't mind, you can get back to whatever it was you were doing out there in the streets and I can get back to packing."

"Let me find out you out here on some petty, hoe shit, ma. You gon' wish you wasn't. I'll make this entire fucking city bleed about what's mine."

After a forceful kiss on the forehead, Ryan finally left and I was able to continue packing. This nigga had some nerve, telling me I was the one being sneaky. There was no telling what he was out there doing, and frankly, I didn't care anymore.

After the most peaceful four hour drive, Keon and I finally made it to Gatlinburg. Our cabin was absolutely beautiful. Not only was it spacious, but it was fully loaded and stocked with food. We were able to book this last minute and we were lucky to get it.

"Look at this place, Keon. It is beautiful and so peaceful. I needed this. Charlotte was getting too toxic and stressful as fuck."

"Who you telling? At least you still got your man. I might be single now."

"We can be single together."

"Mizzy, let's not even think about our broken love lives. Let's unpack so we can do some retail therapy and come back and get in this hot tub and drink ourselves to sleep."

"Sounds good."

Keon and I took the next hour to unpack and get our cabin in order for the next few days. Our first stop of the day was shopping in Gatlinburg at some of our favorite shops to visit as well as Mountain Mall, which was six floors of unlimited shops and sightseeing. This was what I needed, a different environment. I dreamed of being able to have different events all over and Tennessee was high on my list. From the mountains to the forest, this place was beautiful. I could picture all the outdoor events I could plan.

Right now, I was in one of the local candle shops, browsing and enjoying all that this place had to offer. I was truly obsessed with candles, so I was really at peace right now.

After about twenty minutes of being in the shop, I looked down at my phone, noticing it was almost time to meet Keon in the food court for dinner. Although we had a fully stocked kitchen back at the cabin, neither of us wanted to cook on our first night in Tennessee.

I was finally able to decide on a few candles and made my way to the front to check out. I made my purchase and headed toward the food court. The place wasn't extremely packed, which made it easier to walk around the mall.

"Excuse me."

"Damn, watch where you walking."

"My bad, damn. You don't gotta be so damn rude."

"You need to watch where you walking instead of having your head in your phone."

After picking up my phone and making sure my screen wasn't cracked, I looked up, ready to curse this man out because, clearly, he didn't know who he was talking to. I may not have been from around here, but I wasn't going to have anyone think it was OK to disrespect me in any type of way.

"Obviously, you can't hear very well because I did apologize for bumping into you. Now it's up to you if you choose to accept my apology or not, but what you won't do is speak to me like I'm a child. Now, I apologize for bumping into you, but you need to learn how to speak to people."

"Obviously, you can't hear very well. Pay attention to where the fuck you're going. You in this crowded ass place and walking with your head down, bumping into people."

"Nigga, fuck you and go to hell. You talking to me like I'm supposed to be scared of you and shit. Nigga, I ain't one of these local bitches you can talk to any kind of way and run away. You can kiss my ass, stupid ass."

Before he had the chance to say anything, I turned on my heels and headed to my destination. I didn't know what his intentions were, but I didn't have time to find out. All I knew was that I was on vacation and didn't have time for anybody to try to ruin it.

Keon "Ke" Preston

"What we doing tonight? I know we are not going to spend this beautiful night in this hot tub."

"Whatever you want to do is fine with me."

"Keon, what's wrong with you? You were fine at dinner and on the drive back home. What's happened between then and now?"

"You know this nigga didn't even have the balls to text me none today. I walked out on his ass at the restaurant and he didn't even try to stop me. What the hell is that all about?"

"Keon, you don't see me stressing over a text or call from Ryan. Fuck that nigga. You need to have the same mindset about Malik."

"I know that, but I can't help but feel like I have been played for so long. If he wasn't comfortable in his sexuality, he should have never taken it there with me."

"I agree, but you also have to understand where he is coming from. It's not easy for him to be open about his sexuality. Especially with the type of work he does. You shouldn't stress yourself out about this. If it's meant to be, y'all will work it out."

"You're right, Mizzy. I guess I should tell you that Zakari asked me to dinner when we get back to Charlotte."

"Keon, bitch, why are you just now telling me this?"

"I don't know. Before we left today, we met up so that he could give me the contracts for the upcoming photoshoots he wanted me to work with him on and he just asked me to dinner."

"And what did you say?"

103

"I told him no at first."

"At first?"

"Yeah, I told him I was dealing with a situation right now. He told me he respected that and that he still wanted to take me out. I told him I would let him know when I get back in town."

"So, what are you going to do?"

"That's just it, I don't know. I don't know if I am single or still in a relationship or what. I am so lost on all of this shit."

"Keon, how do you feel? This situation with Malik right now needs time to cool off. Now, I'm not saying go out there and start a new relationship, but don't stop living life. The man asked you out to dinner, so go. It's just dinner. Plus, y'all will be working with each other, so don't make shit awkward."

I had to admit my sister was right. I needed to have a

conversation with Malik, but right now was not the right time. I was still in my feelings about what he said to me the other night, so I still needed time to cool off. Thinking about it, there wouldn't be any harm in having dinner with Zakari. Like Mizzy said, we would be working together a lot and I don't want anything to ruin this opportunity for me.

"You're right, sis. I just need to get out of my head and go with the flow."

"Yep. Now let's get dressed and hit up the club. I need to bounce this ass on somebody's son."

"Yassss, bitch! You know I'm twerking all night."

Finishing the last of our wine, we both got out of the hot tub and headed to our rooms to get ready for the club. The clubs in Tennessee always stayed packed, so I knew I wanted to be comfortable but cute. Looking through my luggage, I decided on a pair of red leather shorts from Fashion Nova and paired them with a white, red and green polo short-sleeved shirt with white and red Alex McQueen sneakers. The vibe I was going for was comfortable, yet trendy. I really wanted to tap in to both my feminine and masculine side and I think I did that with this outfit. I decided to pull my locs back into a low bun. My silver studded earrings, matching nose ring, choker and Apple watch were my accessories for the night. I took a few pictures and posted them on my social media accounts. I may have been sad and heartbroken but I didn't have to look that way.

An hour and a half later, we pulled up to one of our favorite clubs and took advantage of the valet parking because we both looked too fine to be walking and waiting in line. Walking into the club, it was jumping. There were dancers at every corner, doing tricks on the poles. The dance floor was packed and everybody was rapping along with Cardi B as "Tomorrow" by GloRilla and Cardi B played throughout the club. Mizzy and I sat at the bar area while we waited for the bartender to come and take our order.

"This shit live tonight. Here, hold my bag. Order me a Patrón and Sprite, I'm about to go bounce this ass real quick. Show these bitches how we do it the Queen City."

I grabbed Mizzy's clutch from her and watched as she made her way to the crowded dance floor, bouncing nothing but ass. All eyes were on my baby sister as she showed out. I sat at the bar and yelled as I hyped my sister up. I was yelling so loud on top of the already loud music, I didn't hear the bartender ask me what I wanted until I felt someone tap me on my shoulder. I turned around in my chair so fast, you could feel the wind from my locs. As soon as I made my way around to see who had the audacity to be tapping on me, I was face to face with Zakari. What the hell? Did this nigga follow me out of the state? So many thoughts ran through my head in that one moment, my words were stuck.

"You look surprised to see me, Keon."

"I mean, yeah, I'm surprised. What are you doing in Tennessee?"

"I flew down with my cousin. After we met up today, he called me and asked if I wanted to fly down, so I said yeah. I wasn't doing shit else. I wanted to check out a couple of venues and a few models I would eventually like to work with."

"Oh OK, how long you staying?"

"We fly back out the day after tomorrow. I got a paper due for class next week."

Before I could say anything, Mizzy came back to the bar, fanning herself. I grabbed one of the napkins and gave it to her so she could wipe the sweat from her face. Before I could say anything, the look on Mizzy's face changed drastically. She looked like she had just seen a ghost, or someone she thought she would never see again.

"The fuck, nigga, you following me? You trying to get your ass cussed out again?" I stood up behind Mizzy as she stood toe to toe with some man I had never seen before. How the fuck did she know this man?

"My'Zariah, who is this man?"

"Some nigga who tried to get disrespectful with me in the mall today. Nigga's mouth was too slick. I don't take that slick talking shit from niggas in Charlotte; what makes anybody think I'm taking that shit from another nigga, regardless if I'm in his city or not?"

I was so caught up with Mizzy, I didn't even get the chance to get a good look at the man, but lord, he was fine. He stood there with a smirk on his face, but despite how good looking he was, I would light this club up behind my sister.

"My'Zariah, what's up, girl? Why are you going off on my cousin like that? How do y'all know each other?"

"Your cousin?" Mizzy and I asked in unison. This really was a small fucking world.

108

My'Zariah "Mizzy" Preston

Here I was, in the middle of the club, going off on this man I didn't even know. Come to find out, he was cousins with Zakari. I was still confused as to why Zakari was in Tennessee, and in the same club as me and Keon. I was a bitch who didn't do well with being disrespected, especially if you didn't know me. When I saw this man in the club tonight, I was reminded of how he tried to handle me in the mall earlier, so my first instinct was to go off on his ass again. Yeah, some may say I was doing too much and to just let it go, but I was caught up in the moment.

"Zakari, what are you doing here?"

"Like I was telling Keon, I flew down with my cousin to look at a few spots for some upcoming photoshoots I have."

"And this is the cousin you came with?"

"Yes. Mizzy and Keon, this is my cousin, Jadarius."

"Nice to meet you both, but you can call me JD." The man I now knew as Jadarius or JD extended his hand out to me, then Keon. I was hesitant at first, but I extended my hand back to him. With me going off on the man both times, I never realized just how fine he was. He stood every bit of six feet tall. His brown skin complexion glowed under the club lights. When he smiled, he had the prettiest set of white teeth. A man with a perfect smile was a big turn on to me. I now stood there like a fool with my eyes glued to this man.

"Can I have my hand back? I don't need you to try to break my fingers."

I quickly removed my hand from his before going over to the bar to have a seat. Keon was so caught up with his conversation with Zakari, he wasn't paying me any attention.

"Do you mind if I have a seat beside you? You're not going to chop my head off, are you?"

"No, you can have a seat. I'm cool. I said what I had to say."

"Yeah, you have, but I want to apologize for earlier. You did apologize for bumping into me and I should have left it at that, so you had every right to feel how you felt. But in all honesty, I didn't mean to disrespect you in any way."

"It's all good. No hard feelings."

"Can I buy you a drink?"

"Sure. Patrón and Sprite, please."

I turned around to face the dance floor as the DJ played "I Just Wanna Rock" by Lil Uzi Vert. The people on the dance floor went crazy over that song, with the majority of them doing the viral TikTok dance to the song. I honestly didn't get the hype about the song, but it was going crazy in the clubs and all over social media.

"Here you go. Patrón and Sprite."

"Thank you." I took the drink out of JD's hand and took a sip, allowing the burn from the liquor and the Sprite to go down.

" So, how do you know my cousin?"

"Zakari and I go to school together. I met him on campus and we became instant friends. He cool as fuck. Real laid back and chill."

"Yeah, he is. Definitely one of my favorite cousins. I see him and your friend know each other as well."

"Keon is my brother, and yes, they do. Kari was looking for a makeup artist for one of his photoshoots he was doing and I told him about Keon, so they have worked together before. And from what Keon was telling me, they are planning to do a few more shoots together soon."

"That's what's up. So, besides school, what do you do? If you don't mind me asking. I don't want to overstep or no shit like that."

"It's OK, I am an event and wedding planner. I own my own business."

"Really, your own business? So you do like birthday parties and stuff like that?"

"Yeah, I do all types of parties, not just birthdays, but anniversary, baby showers and everything."

"Damn, beauty, brains, and a go getter. That shit is sexy."

"So, are you from Charlotte as well?"

"Yeah, born and raised."

"What do you do?"

"I own a few businesses. That's actually why I am out here looking at a couple of buildings to buy and turn into a few more businesses."

"So you are trying to expand beyond Charlotte?"

"I already have. I own businesses and apartment complexes in the Carolinas, Georgia, and Florida. I hope your nigga ain't around, lurkin' at us, sitting here, having a drink."

"If my man was around here, would you care?"

"So you do got a man?"

"I didn't say that, I just asked hypothetically."

"Honestly, no, I wouldn't care. It's just a drink and a friendly conversation."

The more JD talked, the more intrigued I was. He screamed boss energy to the fullest. The more he talked, the more intrigued I was with him. We continued to make small talk about life and our careers, and before I knew it, it was going on two o'clock and the DJ was calling for the last call. While everyone rushed to the bar, JD and I moved

114

closer to the door where Keon and Zakari had been standing for the longest to beat the crowd. I didn't want the conversation to end. I couldn't say the last time I actually had a decent conversation with anyone other than Keon. Even with Ryan, our talks were dry. He was so busy doing whatever it was he was doing to spend any time with me and I was completely over it and over him. I was so at peace with not being around him, I didn't even bother to check my phone for any texts or missed calls from him.

"Keon, are you ready to go? I am trying to beat the crowd out of the parking lot."

"Yes, 'cause I need my beauty rest. I don't wake up this fine."

I rolled my eyes at my brother because lord knows Keon was so extra, but I was going to always stick beside him.

"It was nice meeting you, JD, and thank you for the drinks and the talk. I hope to see you around Charlotte."

"Charlotte is not that big, so I am pretty sure we will have a few run-ins."

115

Moments later, Keon and I were on our way back to the cabin we were staying in. Tonight had really been a great night. It may have started off as a rocky night, however, it ended really well. I was so glad we decided to take this impromptu trip.

Zakari (Kari) White

The last person I expected to run into was Keon. I knew he said he was going out of town, but who could have known it would be in Tennessee? Anyone could see the attraction I had to Keon. From the moment he walked into my studio, I sensed nothing but positive energy coming from him. He was someone I wouldn't mind building something with. I was instantly drawn to him physically. I wasn't afraid to shoot my shot at all, but I wanted to do it on my terms. My last relationship ended pretty badly. I was depressed and closed off from everyone for so long because of the way things ended. I was humiliated and I felt played and betrayed by the one man who was supposed to love me unconditionally. It took me a long time, but I was finally healed from that and ready to date again.

I could sense that Keon was a little nervous around me, but when I asked him out to dinner, that was when he finally said he had a little situation going on. I wasn't trying to make him nervous, but I did want him to know that I found him very attractive. When he told me he basically had someone, I decided to back off, but seeing him in this club had to be some type of sign that maybe we could try to get to know each other on a different level.

"I hope me being here isn't creeping you out. I promise I am not some stalker or anything."

"No, Kari, I'm cool. I'm glad you're here."

"Really? Does that mean you're going to take me up on my dinner offer?"

"I have thought about it."

"Look, I am not trying to interfere with any situation you got going on, so I understand if you're not comfortable with us having dinner together."

"It's not that I don't feel comfortable, it's just that my partner and I had a big fight, so I don't really know where we are at this point."

"I understand completely. If you don't mind me asking, do

you think it's something you both can work out?"

"I'm not sure, honestly. He has a lot he has to deal with personally, so until he can figure himself out, I think it's best for us to have some time apart."

"Is that why you decided to take this mini vacation?"

"You can say that, but Mizzy and I try to go out of town a few times a year, just the two of us."

"That's what's up. Y'all are really close, I can see that."

"Yeah, we are. But what about you? How long have you been single?"

"For about a year. Me and my ex were together for five years, and he was unfaithful for four of those years. I was blind to everything. At first, I thought it was all my fault for not being around, but I was trying to get my business up and running, plus school. It was hard on me at first."

"Four years of infidelity is wild. And you didn't suspect

anything?"

"Not at all at first. We still dated, he still answered his phone when I called or texted, and would be home at a decent time, so I had no reason to suspect anything for a long time."

"So what changed?"

"We would be out in public and he would get distant, like he would walk a little ahead of me. It was little things that I began to notice, but the biggest was the late-night phone calls and sneaking out. I started putting two and two together and eventually, all of my detective work proved my suspicions."

"Damn, Zakari, sorry you had to go through that."

"Thank you, I appreciate that."

It took a while for me to talk about my ex and our breakup, but I felt comfortable with it now. For a while, I just kept to myself. If I wasn't working or going to class, I was home, all alone, moping. I would often talk to Mizzy about it and that was how we became such good friends. She was always so understanding and encouraging. She would tell me a little about her own relationship, which sounded a little similar to mine, but I always told her don't do anything drastic until you have solid proof."

"Well, it looks like Mizzy and JD are getting along better."

"I see that. I am glad 'cause I was ready to give your cousin the business behind my sister." We both laughed, but I knew for a fact he was dead ass serious. The last thing I wanted was any beef with anybody. Especially with Mizzy and Keon.

"So, what do you and Mizzy have planned for tomorrow?"

"Not sure. We didn't really plan anything. This trip was really just spur of the moment."

"Well, since I can't get my dinner with you, how about breakfast in the morning with me, you, and Mizzy? I am not sure what my cousin has planned."

"That sounds good. I will run it by my sister, but I am sure she would be down for it."

Keon and I kicked it a little bit longer before it was time for the club to close. Whenever you heard the DJ yell, "Last call for alcohol," you already knew the crowd was going to get crazy trying to get to the bar.

I hoped we could make this breakfast happen. It wasn't the dinner date I was hoping for, but it was a little more time with him.

Jadarius (JD) White

"So, cuzzo, tell me what you know about My'Zariah?"

"What you wanna know? I mean, she real cool and about her business. We have had a lot of conversations, but nothing too deep or shit like that. Why you asking?"

"She is a feisty one, I can tell."

"JD, you trying to dodge my question. Why are asking about Mizzy? Didn't I see y'all at the bar, having a conversation? Why didn't you find out what you wanted to know then?"

"She got a man?"

"JD, the fuck is this, twenty-one questions or something?"

"Hell yeah, nigga, this twenty-one questions. Now answer, nigga. Who is her man?"

"I don't know who her man is. I never asked her."

"So she do got a man?"

"I don't know what her current relationship status is. Last time she said anything, they were having some issues, but we didn't get too deep into it."

"Ain't no way a nigga fumble a bitch that fine if she is single."

"But ain't you the one always saying women are a distraction when it comes to business and money? That's your motto, right?"

"I know what I said. I ain't trying to marry the girl. She real feisty, I like that shit."

"Nigga, what? So you trying to add her as one of the many females you fucking?"

"First of all, she don't seem like the type. She is too fine for that."

"So, what you saying, you trying to get to know her? What if she does have a man? I know you not trying to mess up a happy home."

"She can't be too happy, she out here having drinks and conversations with me."

"What you mean, JD? Me and Mizzy talk and shit all the

124

time. You're not making sense right now."

"Kari, now nigga, you know you don't want her. You checking for her brother, so y'all talks and conversation is on a whole other level."

"Nigga, you are one confused motherfucker and that's coming from me, the gay cousin."

"Nah, cuzzo, I'm not confused. I know what I like and I like that feisty shit."

Damn, I needed to know more about My'Zariah. To say she was fine was an understatement. Lil mama was beautiful. Most females I fucked with always had a face full of makeup and weave down to their ass crack, but lil mama was on her natural shit. You could tell she had hair just as long as the weave these bitches be wearing, but she had it pulled up into a puff that was beautiful. If she had on makeup, I couldn't tell because she had this natural glow about her. I was interested, and whenever I became interested in something or someone, I didn't stop until I had what I wanted.

With her living in Charlotte, and being close with my cousin, this should be an easy task. I just had to make sure not to scare her off. She seemed like the type who wanted a man to apply straight pressure behind her and that man was me. The thing was, I had to balance my business with getting this woman.

"Well, if you are really interested in her, I mentioned to Keon about maybe having breakfast or brunch in the morning. You trying to come through?"

"Nah, I got some business to handle in the morning, but do me a favor. Text him and tell him something came up and you can't do breakfast but dinner would be better and I join y'all."

"Nigga, are you for real? How do you know they don't already have dinner plans?"

"Find out and let me know. Let's roll to the hotel, I'm tired as fuck. I was trying to find me a lil shorty at the club tonight to bring back and put a hurting on her pussy, but My'Zariah got my attention. It was about to be fuck these hoes once I make her mine."

"Fuck, I'll send Keon a text and see what's up with dinner."

"That's why you are my favorite cousin."

"Nah, I'm the only one that goes along with your crazy ass plans."

"Yeah, that too."

I was tired as fuck by the time I made it back to the hotel room, and all I wanted was a shower and to jump in the bed. I had a few meetings that would help me secure a few of the buildings I wanted to purchase. If everything went according to plan, I would be the owner of two new buildings in Tennessee. That was huge for a nigga like me who hustled my way up. I wasn't getting any younger, so now was the time to get all my business in order so I could officially retire from the drug game. I would always be a part of the empire me and my pops built but I would no

126

longer be getting my hands dirty. I was positive that my brother would be just like me when it came to that business. He would be calling all the shots, but I would always be right there to guide him. I was finally able to doze off with thoughts of My'Zariah. Damn, I think she might be the one to finally lock a nigga down.

***

"Well, Mr. White, everything looks good on our end. All you have to do is sign the paperwork and you will be the owner of two new properties."

This shit went smoother than I expected it to go. I just knew when these men saw me, they were going to try everything they could to raise the price, but I was ready to play their game if I needed to. I was a master at negotiation, but luckily for them, I didn't have to use my skills.

I was now headed back to the room to finish packing. I was flying back to Charlotte in the morning and I was hoping to catch up with my cousin to see if he was able to get My'Zariah and her brother to agree to dinner tonight. I didn't want to miss an opportunity to get to know more about her. I pulled out my phone and noticed a text from Kari, letting me know we were good for dinner tonight. That was perfect.

Me: Aye, go ahead and make the reservations for tonight. Everything on me.

Zakari: Any place you trying to go?

Me: Nah, you already know money is not an issue. Find out where my future wife wants to go.

Zakari: Your future wife? Nigga, you don't even know the girl like that.

Me: The plan is to change that.

Zakari: Yeah OK

I needed me and Zakari to be on the same page. He knew more about what she liked and disliked. He could downplay their friendship all he wanted but I knew my cousin. He wasn't really comfortable around many people, but he was real comfortable around My'Zariah and her brother. That was how I knew he was holding out on me. I wasn't trying to do anything drastic at first. Tonight, l would start by getting to know more about her and getting her to open up to a nigga.

My'Zariah "Mizzy" Preston

"Keon, how did I end up included in your dinner plans tonight? I thought y'all were going to breakfast."

"We were supposed to do breakfast, but he texted me and asked if we could change it to dinner. I guess his cousin wanted to join us."

"Oh, I guess."

"Bitch, stop acting like you are not happy that fine ass man is coming with us."

"What is there to be happy about? He is not my man. I barely know him."

"He looked pretty interested in you last night, and you looked really comfortable."

"It was all small talk, nothing too much."

"Well, maybe you need to stop being so damn mean and stubborn and get friendly with the man."

"For what, Keon? You forgot I got a nigga back in Charlotte I can't get rid of?"

"Girl, fuck Ryan. That nigga from last night is a boss. You could just tell by the way he walked, talked, and everything. The man screamed boss energy."

I couldn't help but laugh at Keon. He analyzed people in his own way. The shit was funny to me because he thought he was doing something. I didn't want to tell him that JD owned a few businesses. I would never hear the end of it.

"Well, you're lucky I didn't plan anything else or I wouldn't even be going to this dinner."

"Shit, I don't even know why I agreed, but I think this was all Zakari's doing to get me to have dinner with him since I turned him down."

"Why do you keep turning him down? You can tell he really likes you. The attraction is there from both of y'all."

"How can you tell I am attracted to him?"

"Because I have known you all my life, so I know how you get around a nigga you like."

"Well, My'Zariah, you are wrong. There is no attraction."

I decided not to continue with the conversation; there was no point. I knew my brother and he was only in denial because he was in his feelings about Malik. I understood why because they had long history, so I knew why he was hesitant. I would never tell Keon what to do, but I honestly felt Malik would never get over his fear of being rejected by his family for being gay. I also felt that Keon deserved better, but it wasn't my decision.

The ringing of my phone distracted me from my thoughts. Looking down at my phone, I saw it was Ryan calling. This was the first time he had called since we'd been in Tennessee. I would be lying if I said I wasn't happy about it.

"Hello?"

"What's good, baby girl? When you coming home? Your man missing you like crazy, and I got a surprise for you."

"Ryan, where you at with all that noise? I can barely hear you."

"I'm cutting hair, but answer my question."

"I will be home late tomorrow."

Wherever Ryan was, was so loud, I could barely hear anything he was saying, but I could have sworn I heard a female in the background. It was the audacity for me because it sounded like the bitch was right on his lap. The funny thing was, the voice sounded very familiar, I just couldn't quite make it out though.

132

"Ryan, who is that female?"

"Baby, what female? You hear the TV in the background."

"That is not the fucking TV. The bitch sounds like she right on your fucking lap. You really are on that dumb shit."

"Baby, there is no one in here but me and the dudes who I'm cutting hair for. You hear the TV."

Not even bothering to say anything else, I hung up. I could only imagine what type of surprise he had. My mind kept going back to the female I heard in the background. He tried to play it off like it was the TV, but I knew better. That voice sounded too clear to be coming from a television.

This nigga thought he was slick, but like my mama always said, "What's done in the dark will come to the light." For a while now, I have suspected Ryan was messing around with other women and his poor excuse for a lie just proved it. I would be lying if I said I wasn't in my feelings about it because I never gave the nigga a reason to cheat on me. When I get home, I was packing his shit. I didn't give a fuck how much he begged and cried.

(Later that night)

I really wasn't feeling this dinner tonight but I promised Keon I would go with him. I had to admit, the restaurant had a nice little vibe. It was more like a lounge than a restaurant. The vibe had a 90s aesthetic and they played 90s R&B and hip-hop. Now this was my type of vibe. The club scene was cool at times, but I preferred this type of environment.

"This place is cute, sis."

"Yeah, it's pretty dope. I hope the food is good."

"Mizzy, I am good with some wings and Patrón. I ain't trying to be fancy."

134

Keon and I found a table and waited for JD and Zakari to arrive. I noticed Keon kept checking his phone. I hoped he wasn't talking to Malik. Shit, who was I to judge? I still hadn't told him about Ryan earlier, but my mind was made up. I was ending shit.

The crowd was beginning to get thicker and I was getting very impatient, just waiting here. Granted, it had only been about fifteen minutes, but it was the principle. They asked us out and they were late. What type of shit was that?

Another five minutes went by when I saw JD walk through the building like he owned the place. This man had the smoothest walk; it was like every female in the room stopped just to stare at him. He was dressed so simply in a pair of black, distressed Amiri jeans, a white tee that showed off his tatted arms, and a pair of black and white Jordan 4s that looked like they were fresh out of the box. He was wearing a Jordan hat that covered his hair but I knew he had a crisp line. When we finally made eye contact, I swear I fell in love with his hazel eyes. I never noticed just how sexy his eyes were until now.

Watching as he walked over to where we were, I was thankful I didn't wear the white romper I started to wear because my panties were wet just from watching him walk. That big dick energy was just dripping off this man.

"What's good, beautiful? I hope y'all wasn't waiting too long."

"Only fifteen minutes, so not too long."

"You can thank my cousin for the wait."

"It's all good. This place is nice, so I didn't mind waiting."

"Cool, let's go find a table so I can buy you a drink. Patrón and Sprite, right?"

Not him remembering my drink order from last night. I thought that was really cute of him to remember something so simple.

We followed JD to the back of the restaurant to where they had tables set up. The section only sat two to a table, so JD and I grabbed one while Keon and Kari did the same. That was something else I liked about this place. It had a very private vibe to it, definitely a little date night place.

Not long after finding our seat, our waitress came over to

take our drink orders. Of course, I didn't have to give mine because JD already knew what I wanted.

"This place is cute. What made you decide to come here tonight? I don't take you for an R&B type of nigga. Not that I got a problem with it."

"I fuck with this place heavy. I try to come here at least once when I come down here. They got some good ass wings and hookah."

"I don't know about the hookah, but I guess I got to try the wings if they are as good as you say."

"Take my word for it, lil mama. The hot honey wings are the best flavor. That's if you can handle a little spice."

"I'm good with some heat. I can handle it."

"That's a good thing."

"So, tell me, My'Zariah, you got a man back in Charlotte?"

This was the question I was avoiding. I wasn't one to lie about my relationship status, but what me and Ryan had was over in my eyes and I wasn't in the mood to discuss it, either. I decided to just be upfront with him.

"What I got back at home is nothing worth talking about. I had a dude, but things with us are pretty much over. The games he was playing, I just can't deal with anymore. The love ain't there anymore; it's been fading for a while."

"Damn, sorry to hear that. I hope you don't think all men are like him. I'm not sure what the situation is, but don't let what y'all had turn you bitter toward all men."

"I could never. I am smart enough to know that all men are not like him. Besides Keon, I have another brother who treats women with the utmost respect. Plus, I watched how my grandfather treated my grandmother. He treated her like a queen and still does even after thirty years of marriage."

"Damn, your grandparents have been married for thirty years? That's some real Black love type shit. That's the type of shit I am trying to be on. I want my first marriage to be my last marriage. Shit, I seen both of my parents step out on each other—mostly my dad—so I can't say that I was shown how to properly love a woman, but I do know that I don't ever want to be the man that causes her pain. Seeing my mother cry over my father every night, I swore I would never have my woman cry over me."

"You know about all this, so why are you single?"

"No one has caught my attention until now."

"So I have caught your attention? Why is that?"

"Ain't gon' lie, you beautiful as hell, you got a slick ass mouth, and that shit is sexy. You not gon' let nobody talk to you crazy and I like that. The way you went off on me, any other bitch would have gotten their feelings hurt for coming at me like that."

"So you just assumed I was different?"

"I know you are, and I like that."

"What else do you like?"

"Shit, I'm starting to like you."

"You just met me. I could be some psycho ass stalker, for all you know."

"Shit, that's a risk I'm willing to take. Once I put this dick in your life, you gon' have a reason to stalk me."

"Do you not have a filter?"

"Nah, I don't have a filter, and neither do you, and that shit is sexy. I think we made for each other."

"How are we made for each other? We don't even know each other."

"Well, Mizzy, let's change that. Come hit this dance floor with me and don't be grinding all on my dick, either."

"You and that mouth of yours."

"You trying to see what all this mouth can do?"

"Nigga, please."

As the song switched to "Let Me Hold You" by Omarion and Bow Wow, JD grabbed my hand and led me to the dance floor. We danced along to the song as JD rapped Bow Wow's verse and I sang along with Omarion. Looking into this man's eyes, I had to mentally tell myself not to be weak. I wasn't a cheater, by far, but temptation was getting the best of me. The way I felt, I would gladly give this man some pussy. The song switched to 112's "You Already Know" and JD pulled me in closer and grabbed my ass. Just from the way he squeezed my ass, I was ready to say fuck those wings and head back to the cabin.

"You looking at me like you trying to give me the pussy right here in this club, but I promise you, you're not ready for all that. I'ma different type of nigga. I don't share, and you got a situation at home you got to handle. Now, let's get off this dance floor before I go against my word and take you in one of those bathrooms back there and put something in your life you never had before."

I removed my hands from around JD's neck as he grabbed my hand and led us back to the table. Our food was just coming out and I was glad because I needed to do something other than look at this man.

"I'm trying to tell you these the best wings in the state."

"They good, but mine are better."

"Typical female to say some shit like that."

"Well, I am not your typical female, and I know my way around the kitchen. My grandmother made sure of that."

"I hear you mention your grandmother and grandfather a lot. Where are you parents? If you don't mind me asking."

"No, I don't mind at all. I don't know who my father is. My mother was sixteen when she had me and decided that she did not want to be bothered with a baby and gave me to my grandparents and left. The nigga she said was my dad turned out not to be. She left, only to come in and out of my life when she felt like it. She is here now, and supposedly, she is sick and wants to spend time with me in case she dies."

"Damn, I am sorry to hear that. I hope things work out for her, health wise."

142

"To be honest, I don't really believe her. Mellissa lives for drama and attention. The bitch is up to something, I just feel it. If I am wrong, I will ask God to forgive me, but I don't think I am."

"Maybe she really is sick. Give her the benefit of the doubt."

"I am, but I am on high alert."

"So, Keon is not really your brother?"

"Technically, no, he is my uncle but my grandparents never referred to me as their grandchild. I was always their daughter so I was raised as so. Keon and I are only a few years apart, which is why we are so close."

"Your grandparents sound like great people."

"They are my world."

After finishing up our food and drinks, we decided to head on over to the hookah lounge and continue our night. We were soon joined by Keon and Zakari. We had bottles of Patrón and hookah being passed around for the entire night. Tonight, I was the most relaxed I had been in a while and I was glad we'd decided to come out for our last night. Just thinking about going back home had me a little depressed, but shit, it is what it is. I couldn't run from my problems forever.

My first order of business when I touched back in Charlotte was ending things with Ryan. I knew I had to be strong and not let him get in my head like he did the last time. I had to think about my feelings for a change. If that was selfish, oh well.

Ryan Marshall

"Fuck, girl, just like that. Suck my dick just like that. Spit on it, make that shit nasty. If you want what I got in my pocket, deep throat that shit."

It was one thing this bitch knew how to do and that was give some bomb ass head. My toes were hard and I prayed I didn't get a cramp. She was working for this dope I had for her and I didn't mind giving it to her after this.

"Shit, I'm about to nut. Fuck!"

In a matter of seconds, I spilled all my seeds down this bitch's throat and she sucked it up like it was her favorite ice cream flavor. After a few minutes of me trying to catch my breath, I was able to get myself together. I grabbed my jeans, putting them back on before reaching in my pocket and handing her what she had just worked for.

"My daughter must not be giving you this type of head 'cause this is more than the usual. This will last me a few days."

"Aye, watch your mouth, and don't worry about what me and my girl got going on. You need to worry about fixing y'all relationship 'cause she can't stand the ground you walk on."

"You think I care if the little stubborn ass bitch likes me or not? That's why I gave the little bitch up to my parents because I didn't want to be tied down to a crying ass baby. Hell, I told her ass I had cancer and she didn't even care. Didn't shed not one tear, so I couldn't care less how she feels. The feelings are mutual."

"Why would you lie to her like that? That's some evil ass shit, to make her think you sick and dying. What was the reason?"

"Because my money is running low. I was hoping to get close to the bitch to make her think I was sick to scam some money out of her until I get back right."

"So you just trying to get a come up off your daughter?"

"Yep, and no, I don't feel no way about it."

"You really are one sick ass individual."

"And what the fuck makes you any better, Ryan? You got me sucking you off every other day, but you claim to love Mizzy. Fuck outta here with that. That is some fake ass love."

"Ain't shit fake about me. Mizzy has my heart, so all the love I have for her is real. She gon' be my wife one day. What we got going on is a business deal. I supply your habit, you suck my dick, everyone is happy."

"I can make you even happier if you let me give you some pussy. I know that little bitch ain't fucking you right with all the hoes you fuck with. Word on the street is, Azlea's baby is yours, so how you plan to explain that to Mizzy?"

"Damn, for a dope fiend, you sure know everybody fucking business. That hoe's baby is not mine. That bitch done

147

fucked around with half the fucking city, so ain't no telling who her baby daddy is, but the lil nigga damn sure ain't mine. And as far as you giving me some pussy, I bet the fuck I won't. Bad enough I let you suck my dick. The fuck is wrong with you?"

"Shit, I'm just trying my luck, son-in-law."

This was one delusional ass bitch. The fact that she would think I would stick my dick in her was wild to me. Even if she wasn't Mizzy's mama, I wouldn't fuck her. She was a messy ass bitch who talked too fucking much and didn't have any fucking morals. The fact that she felt comfortable sucking my dick and now trying to give me the pussy was crazy. I wouldn't fuck her with a dildo strapped to me. I was really thinking about cutting this bitch off for good. Shit was getting too close to home.

I was still shook from yesterday when she was being spiteful, talking to me while I was on the phone with Mizzy. Speaking of Mizzy, my baby was due to be home later today and I had a big surprise for my baby. I was ready to make our shit official and ask her to marry a nigga. The fight we had when she tried to leave a nigga had me ready to tie her ass down. I was also tossing those damn birth control pills as well. If I had to tie her ass down with a baby, that was what I was going to do. It was by any means necessary to keep my girl.

148

Right now, I had to get rid of Mellissa. She was over there looking real comfortable and I had to nip that shit in the bud real quick.

"Yo, you got your shit, now you gotta bounce."

"I'll leave, but if you want to keep this little secret between us, I suggest you think twice about cutting me off. I wouldn't mind telling your precious Mizzy how you let me suck your dick in her house."

"Bitch, my girl wouldn't believe shit you say. The way she feels about you, you can tell her the sky is blue and she would call you a liar to your face, so try that shit again."

"Hmmm, you think I'm dumb enough not to have proof of our little encounters, son-in-law? I got recordings and I know about the birthmark on the left side of your dick. The one that is shaped like a heart. Yeah, I notice shit. I need to use the bathroom first."

"You that damn heartless you would tell your own daughter that shit?"

"Like I said, fuck that lil bitch. She don't give a shit about me, so why should I care about her feelings?"

This was one evil ass woman and I was mentally kicking myself for even getting involved with her ass. The shit wasn't even supposed to go as far as it did. When I first met Mizzy, she told me about how her mother left her to be raised by her grandparents and how she had recently started coming in and out of the picture. One day while the two of us were out, we ran into Mellissa, who was back in town for one of her visits. When Mizzy introduced us, she stared at a nigga like she wanted to give up the pussy right then and there.

About a week after that, I ran into her at a kickback one of my homeboys was having. After she spotted me, she was all over me that same night. That was the first time I let her give me some head, and I must admit, that shit was A-fucking-1 from the start. I mean, porn star type head. Soon after, she started asking me if she could credit some dope. A few times, I let her pay me back by sucking me off, and now that shit was like clockwork. I never really got into her relationship with Mizzy, but now I saw she really didn't give a damn about her daughter. The shit was kind of sad, honestly. I really needed to get away from this bitch now and she was trying to blackmail a nigga.

"Look, man, you need to get out. I don't know what time Mizzy is coming back, but you don't need to be here when she comes. You got what you want, plus extra, so just leave, please."

"I will leave, but don't fuck with me, son-in-law. I don't give a fuck about feelings."

"Yo, get the fuck out before you be eating my bullets, stupid bitch."

The bitch tripped over her feet trying to get out of the house so damn fast. I would be a fool to sit here and let that bitch try to blackmail me and ruin what me and Mizzy had. Shit between me and Mizzy was rocky, but on my life, I was getting our shit back on track. I would put a bullet to that bitch before I let her hurt my girl.

I spent the next few hours, making sure this place was perfect for when Mizzy made it back. I even ordered from one of her favorite restaurants. I wanted to make sure everything was perfect for her when I gave her the ring and asked her to marry me. To pass the time, I decided to play a little Madden on the PS5.

An hour later, I heard the alarm to the door go off. I watched as my baby walked through the door. I got up as soon as she walked in so that I could help her with her bags.

"What's up, baby? Let me get your bags for you."

"Thank you, Ryan."

"How was your trip?"

"It was good. Exactly what I needed."

"I'm glad you had a good time. Go ahead and get settled, I got dinner for you, and we need to talk."

"What do we need to talk about, Ryan?"

"Nah, go get yourself comfortable and I will warm your dinner up for you."

I waited around for Mizzy for about thirty minutes until she put her stuff up and headed back into the kitchen where I had her dinner waiting for her. I was nervous as fuck, but like I said when I first met her, she was going to be my future and I put that on everything.

"All right, Ryan, what do we need to talk about?"

"Don't you want to eat first?"

"No, Ryan, I don't want to eat. I just want to take a nap. I ended up driving the entire way back and I am tired."

"All right, look, I know when you left, things between us were rocky and I promised you we were going to get back to the way we were and I meant that. All the late nights and not answering your calls and shit is over, I promise. I am so close to being done with this street life. My homeboy been telling me for a while that he can help me get my shop and I am ready to go for it. I am ready to do this for us. I am ready to start a family with you. My'Zariah, will you do me the honor of marrying me?"

"Ryan, neither one of us is ready for marriage. You are only proposing now because of what happened before I left. No, I won't marry you, and I think we need some time apart. Things between us have not been good for a while and I am tired of masking my feelings."

"Are you fucking serious right now? I am down on one knee like a bitch, asking for your hand in marriage, and all you can say is we need some time apart? What kind of shit is that, Mizzy?"

"Ryan, what gave you any indication that I was ready to get married? This is all on you because your sneaky ass is feeling guilty about something."

"I don't have shit to feel guilty about because I'm not doing shit for me to be guilty."

"And you stand on that lie, Ryan?"

"What lie, Mizzy? Tell me what lie."

"So I'm assuming the same bitch you were with the other day when you called me is the same bitch that left her draws in my bathroom? 'Cause the red thong in the bathroom is too small for me. So start talking, nigga."

"What thong? The only underwear in this house are yours."

154

My fucking heart was racing because there was no way this
bitch had just set me up like this. I was pissed at myself for
even bringing her ass here, but I didn't have anywhere else
to go. I gave up my place a while ago so I was fucked. I
didn't know how I was getting out of this shit, but I
couldn't admit to anything. Shit was going left for me and I
had to fix it. I was getting sick thinking about losing Mizzy.

"Talk, Ryan. There is no need to lie about it. You're caught,
so just admit it. Who the fuck did you have in my house
that she felt comfortable to leave her funky ass underwear
in my bathroom?"

"Baby, I swear I didn't have anyone here. I'm not fucking
around with anyone, you have to believe me."

"I don't believe shit you're saying. Get your shit and leave
now, while I am calm. You already know how I get down,
so get the fuck out of my house. Take that cheap ass ring
back wherever you got it from and get your money back. I
am done and I mean that."

Feeling defeated, I grabbed my keys and left. I refused to
take anything else with me because what we had would
never be over. I just needed to give Mizzy some time to
cool off so we could have an actual conversation. I wasn't
confessing to anything but I was damn sure prepared to beg
for my woman. For the last few years, Mizzy had been my

155

rib. I knew I had been fucking up for the last few months but her finding out never crossed my mind. I needed to get my shit together, but first, I needed to find Mellissa cause I was killing that bitch. On everything, I was making her a distant memory.

Jadarius (JD) White

"What's good, nigga?"

"Ain't shit, big brother, just coolin'. What's good with you?"

"Shit, same. Come fuck with me at my house, I got some business to discuss with you."

"Aight, give me an hour. I got a shorty I'm trying to fuck with real quick."

"Tae, make plans with that hoe later and come on through."

I was back home in Charlotte but I had yet to get back to work. Shit, a nigga was tired as fuck from being in Tennessee the last few days, but I was happy as fuck that the trip wasn't a waste. I was now the owner of two new properties. I knew one would be my future gun shop. I'd wanted a gun shop for as long as I could remember. I wanted the shop to also have a gun range connected to the back.

I was thinking about giving the other building to Zakari as a photo studio. That man was a beast with a camera and all that editing and photography shit. I'd seen him make some of the ugliest motherfuckers look damn good in magazines and shit. Truth be told, I had wanted to do something big for my cousin for a while. He really was one of the realest out there. A lot of our other family members used to give him slack because of his sexuality, but I made sure to shut that shit down every time. I never understood why people had to voice their opinion on how someone chose to live their life. I knew I loved pussy so the shit never bothered me. As long as no one ever tried me like that, I was good with it.

I waited around for another thirty minutes before I saw my brother's car pull up on the camera outside. I wasn't surprised when I saw he had that nigga Ryan with him. They were joined at the fucking hip, it seemed. You didn't see one without the other. I was glad he came, though, because he could also benefit from this discussion.

158

"JD, what's so important I had to cancel my plans, bruh?"

"Nigga, what I tell you? Money first, nigga. Now, whatever hoe you was trying to fuck on, can wait."

"I'm here now, nigga, so what's up?"

"What's up with that nigga Ryan, out there in the car, looking like he just lost his best friend and shit? He needs to bring his ass in here to handle this business with his shop. Nigga hit me up about finally taking me up on my offer and he out there looking lost."

"Dummy done fucked up with his girl and she kicked his ass out last night. Nigga been at my house since last night."

"That's his own fucking fault. Nigga put random bitches before his woman and his money. I don t have no sympathy for him at all. Y'all lil niggas gon' learn one day."

"Y'all? Big bro, you already know I'm all about my money."

"Well, fuck it. If he wants to stay out there and look like a sad puppy, that's on him. We got business to discuss."

I was done trying to school these boys. It was too much money out there to keep babysitting grown ass men.

"So, what you needed to talk about?"

"Well, you know I was in Tennessee for a few days. I was able to secure two more buildings. Everything secured and in my name."

"That's what's up, JD. So what's the plan? What you trying to do with them?"

"I was thinking about renting one of them out to Zakari as his studio. Nigga been saying he wanted a studio out in Tennessee for the longest."

"Yeah, he has been, but what about the other one?"

"Nigga, I am finally getting my gun shop. I was thinking about getting a little condo out there for a while until I get

160

my shop up and running the way I want it."

"So what does that have to do with me, JD?"

"Johntae, what you mean? You about to take over shit sooner than expected, my nigga. I need you to be on your shit. I won't be here to hold your hand anymore. If you really want this shit, it's time to get focused and get your mind right."

"Jadarius, I have been doing this shit for a while now. My team is solid and money is still flowing like it should. Hell, better, if I'm being honest. Stop being so paranoid. Go get one of them hoes you fuck with and get you some pussy and calm your overly paranoid ass down."

"Aight, lil nigga. You say you ready and don't need me, we will see."

"JD, you are too uptight. Let me hook you up with one of these freaks that be at the club. I am talking bad ass bitches who don't mind doing more than just dancing."

"Fuck no, nigga. I'm not putting my dick nowhere on none of them low budget ass strippers. I like my women natural.

Plus, I met someone while I was in Tennessee. Lil mama is beautiful too."

"So that's the reason you trying to get down there so fast. I thought it was money before pussy, nigga."

"Nah, it ain't shit like that. She is actually from Charlotte; she was down there on vacation with her people and shit. She knows Kari from school and whatnot."

"Nigga, you not about to get serious with nobody. She probably just another fuck to add to your roster."

"She ain't nothing like that."

"Well, big brother, like you tell me, don't get caught slipping and forget what's important. Stay focused."

"I see you got jokes. But you better focus on getting your team right. Looks like your right hand is about to lose his shit out there."

"Man, fuck that nigga. I'm about to drop his ass off at

Azalea's house. I ain't up for that depressed shit from this nigga."

"Who is his girl, anyway?"

"Shit, I don't even know. I only saw her like once, but I don't be all in that man business like that."

"Yeah, I feel you."

"But aight, my boy. I'm out, and trust me, I got this shit. I was born to hustle, remember that."

I watched as my brother drove off before heading back to my room. I needed to get my plans ready to get my store off the ground. I took most of my day just researching different guns as well as the basics of owning and operating a gun shop. I was determined to make this my next franchise, just like my apartment complex and clubs. I never wanted to be that nigga who was in the streets all my life. I wanted to make it out early and made sure that me and my family would always have income coming in. Once I left the game, I was never going back to it. That was another reason why I never tried to fall in love. I didn't need that distraction. When the time was right, I wanted my woman to know that she only had to work if she wanted to.

As her man, it would always be my job to take care of the family I created.

After another few hours of studying and research, I decided to hit Mizzy up to see if she wanted to grab something to eat. I knew she said she had a little situation, but I didn't give a fuck. I was feeling her sexy ass and I wanted to see her.

Me: What's good beautiful? What you got going on tonight?

Mizzy: I don't have anything planned.

Me: Shit I'm trying to take you out. What's up?

Mizzy: That's fine we can go out.

Me: Shit shoot me your location and I will pick you up around eight.

Mizzy: OK!

What I was about to do was out of the norm for me. I couldn't remember the last time I took a girl out on a date. All that wining and dining shit was not for me, but with Mizzy, I would have to step my game up and be on my grown man dating shit because lil mama was different and not like these other broads. I could tell that just from the little time I spent with her. She comes from strong, Black love, and I have to approach her differently.

My'Zariah "Mizzy" Preston

"You OK, boo?"

"Yeah, I'm good, Keon. More pissed than anything. This man really had the nerve to have a bitch in my house. How dumb can you get? I am just mad at myself for not setting up these cameras before I left so I could see who the hoe was."

"You should have picked up the nearest extension cord and beat his ass with it. How disrespectful can he be? And I bet the bitch looks like Kermit the frog."

"I wasn't even that mad. I'd had my suspicions about the nigga for some time now. And to top it off, he had the nerve to ask me to marry him with that cheap ass ring. The

166

fuck type of shit is that?"

"Bitch, not the cheap ring. I know you lying."

"Ring look like it came out of a kiosk in Walmart."

"I sure hope you not sitting around all day. crying and moping around behind Ryan. You need me to come and help pack his shit? You know I keep trash bags handy."

"Yeah, you can come help me tomorrow. I got a date tonight."

"Bitch, you just became single less than twelve hours ago. Who are you going on a date with?"

"JD texted me and asked me to dinner."

"I still can't believe him and Zakari are cousins. Good looks run in that family for sure."

"That is crazy that they are related. And it's just dinner, so nothing serious."

"You need to enjoy yourself, sis. Don't let Ryan occupy your mind. I know it's hard, but you can't mope around all day."

"Well, if it ain't the pot calling the kettle black, Keon. You need to have that same energy with Zakari and Malik. Zakari really likes you and you giving him the cold shoulder."

"I'm not giving him the cold shoulder, but I honestly don't know where Malik and I stand at the moment."

"I understand that. Has Malik tried to reach out to you, or have you tried reaching out to him?"

"No, and I shouldn't be the one reaching out. I am not the one with the problem."

"That's true, but you can at least try to get to the bottom of why he is feeling how he is feeling and maybe make some type of compromise."

"There is no compromise. I am not a bitch you keep hidden from the world. I like to be shown off."

"Well, Keon, Zakari is a photographer; he would love to show you off."

"You're not helping me, Mizzy."

"Ke, you know I love you, but you gotta stand your ground with him. If y'all can't come together and compromise, then what y'all had has expired and it's time to move on. Not everyone is here to stay, some are only here for a season."

"I understand, sis, and I have a lot of things I need to sort out. But you go and enjoy your night and call me the minute you walk in the house. And take your gun, niggas are crazy."

"I will. I love you and I'll text you when I get home."

I hung up with Keon and decided to give my mama a call. I hadn't spoken to her since the last time I was over there and that wasn't like me. I was used to talking to her every day, sometimes multiple times a day.

I grabbed my drink and dialed up my mama. The first thing I needed to do was apologize to her for being disrespectful in her house. My grandmother was old school, so she still had a landline phone and an answering machine. She did not fuck with cell phones whatsoever.

I let the phone ring four times until the answering machine picked up. I wasn't leaving a message so I decided to call my daddy to see where my mama was. Unlike my mama, my daddy loved his cell phone. We all pitched in and got him an iPhone. He loved that damn phone because he was able to watch his games and keep up with all the baseball and football scores.

"Hello?"

"Hey, Daddy."

"Well, hey. If it ain't my baby girl. How you doing?"

"I'm OK, Daddy. How are you?"

"I'm doing good for an old man, I reckon."

"You're not old, Daddy. Where is Mama at?"

"She is out shopping with your sister and Mellissa. And I heard what happened between you and Mellissa and I don't blame you for nothing. Nobody can tell you how to feel when it comes to the relationship with your birth mama. Now, I love my daughter Mellissa just as much as I love the rest of my kids, including you, but I told her a long time ago that if she kept coming in and out of your life, you would grow to hate her. I prayed for it not to happen, but it did. I can't fault you for how you feel and I will be damned if I let anyone else."

"Thank you, Daddy. I needed to hear that."

"You're welcome, baby. Now I will tell your mama to call you. I am watching the game highlights. I love you, baby girl."

"I love you, too, Daddy."

I hung up with my daddy, feeling better than I had felt since all this shit went down. I could always count on my daddy to lift my spirits and make me feel better. I still had a

171

little more time to spare before my date, so I grabbed the remote and browsed Netflix until I found something to watch.

(later that night)?

Tonight, we decided to go to a local seafood restaurant here in Charlotte called The Crab Cracker. It was one of my favorite places to go because they had the best cajun shrimp and lobster tails in the city. I was glad he chose a place that wouldn't be overly crowded and would allow us to just vibe and continue getting to know one another.

I pulled up to the restaurant and sent him a text, letting him know I was here. Of course, he hadn't arrived yet, so I decided to just sit in my car and wait. I wanted to see when he pulled up. I waited for another five minutes before JD sent me a text, letting me know he was pulling in. I waited until he got out before I did the same and met him. He was dressed simply, yet looked so damn good in a pair of red Nike sweats with the matching hoodie and red and white high top Dunks. I always said how fine Ryan was but JD was on a different level. He had street swag and was casual all at the same time. He was one of those men social media talked about being able to switch their style up. I blew my horn so I could get out and catch up to him so we could walk in together.

"You look good."

"Thank you, JD, so do you."

"Stop looking so nervous, girl. I'm not gon' bite you, it's dinner. But if you trying to be dessert, just say the word."

"What?"

"Shit, you looking at me like you trying to get ate."

"I'm ready to eat, not get ate, so can we please go in?"

"Yeah, come on. I'm not trying to scare you off."

I followed as JD led us into the building. Thankfully, it wasn't crowded and we were seated right away. We asked for a seat in the back, away from the little crowd that they did have. Like a true southern gentleman, JD pulled my seat out and allowed me to order first.

"You having your usual Patrón and Sprite?"

173

"No, not tonight. I'll just have water with lemon."

We both ordered drinks and food and talked the entire time. I listened as he told me all about the business he owns and his gun shop he was working on. To say he grew up hustling, he was super smart. Not only does he have his associate's degree, but his master's as well. I was really impressed just by listening to him.

"You have accomplished a lot in such a short time. How did you find the time?"

"When I wasn't in the streets or with my pops, I was in the books or in the classroom. A lot of niggas spend their free time in the clubs and bars. I have always known I wanted to get out early so I worked toward that goal."

"I feel you. My event company is my major goal. I am already doing events but I want a store front. A few, actually. I want my clients to come in to my store front and look at the many ideas I have on display and be able to sit down and have a conversation with me and my staff about what they envision for their special day."

"So, what are you doing to accomplish that vision?"

"Well, I am in school for business and design."

"OK, have you researched where you want your shops to be located, or how you want the aesthetic of your shop to look like? You said you want multiple, right?"

"Yeah, I do."

"OK, have you researched what states you want them in? Do you want them all in North Carolina?"

"No, I haven't thought about all of that."

"Then you don't have a clear vision, love. You have ideas, but in order for it to be a clear vision, you have to have your plan written out and every detail mapped out."

"I never thought of it like that."

"Keep fucking with me and I got you. If you want, one day, I will show you my notebook with all the visions of my business, including my gun shop."

"I would really like that."

We sat and talked up until it was closing time, and just like our time in Tennessee, I wasn't ready for it to end. I was really starting to enjoy his company more and more.

"Damn, they had to literally kick us out of there." I laughed, thinking about how annoyed the waitress looked with us. We were the last people in there, besides the staff, and they were looking at us hard, waiting for us to leave.

"Them people was ready to get the hell on out of there."

"I had a really good time, JD. Thank you. Shit has been crazy since I got back in Charlotte."

"What happened?"

"Let's just say my suspicions were right about my boyfriend. I found a pair of underwear in my bathroom and shit went left with us."

"Damn, love, I am sorry to hear that. I hate you had to go through that. Some men just don't know how to handle a good woman."

"Well, he damn sure didn't."

"Shoot me your address, and tomorrow, I will come through and we will start getting those ideas mapped out."

Before I had a chance to answer, I heard my name being called. I was annoyed at this point, because who would have the audacity to be calling my name like that? I turned around to see who it was, only for it to be my sister, Kelsey, and Mellissa.

"Look at my beautiful baby. I have been trying to reach you."

"Reach me for what?"

"My treatments start soon and I wanted to have dinner or lunch with you."

"I will think about it, Mellissa."

"Mizzy, why are you being rude? Aren't you going to introduce me to your boyfriend?"

She was being so fucking annoying. The last thing I wanted to do was introduce her to anyone.

"Mellissa, this is JD. JD, this is Mellissa, my birth mother, and my sister, Kelsey."

JD just nodded while Mellissa stood there, looking lost.

"I thought your boyfriend was. Well, that's what Kelsey told me."

"Mellissa, don't piss me off, and Kelsey, stop telling my fucking business. Y'all can go now. I am about to go home."

They both knew I was getting angry so they turned around

and headed in the direction they came from. Kelsey was one dumb girl. Mellissa didn't care for anybody and I would bet my last dollar she was using her for something.

"I'm sorry about that."

"What you apologizing for?"

"Them."

"No need to apologize, you didn't do anything."

"She just gets under my skin, and my sister Kelsey is so stupid, she doesn't realize she is being used."

"We need to get on up out of here. And don't think I forgot about you sending me your address."

I sent him my address and we both prepared to leave. Despite the unexpected guests, tonight was another great night. JD was definitely someone I was beginning to love spending time with.

Ryan Marshall

I was fucking going through it. I had been calling and texting My'Zariah for the past two days and nothing. I knew she didn't have my number blocked because the messages on my iPhone were still blue. I was thankful she was still able to see my messages. I was literally sick, thinking about the possibility of us not being together. It was stupid of me to keep thinking I could keep fucking up and not have shit blow up in my face.

I had been staying at Azela's house for the last two days and the shit was getting annoying. Out of all times, she had her son home, and all that lil nigga did was cry. She didn't know what to do with him because she never had him. I was glad she took him back to her mama's house because all that crying was giving me a migraine.

"Good morning, baby daddy."

"Man, gon' 'head with that dumb shit. I am really not in the mood. Fuck around and get your feelings hurt."

"Nigga, you in my house. You don't have to be here."

"Man, fuck all that. I done told you to stop trying to pin that baby on me. Go find that nigga that nutted in you to make that child."

"Why are you even here? 'Cause all you have done is lay on my couch, looking lost. That hoe got you that sprung?"

"What are you even talking about?"

"Your bitch must have kicked you out because you ain't never stayed this long. So either y'all had a huge fight or she flat out kicked you out."

"Stay the fuck out my business, yo."

"Yeah, she kicked your ass out, huh? Man, I don't understand y'all niggas. Y'all fuck up and cheat on your bitch, and when shit comes to the light, you walk around, looking like a sick dog. How you claim you love her but all you been doing is cheating on her? All y'all motherfuckers know how to do is lie, cheat, and fuck up. Y'all don't know shit about love or loving a woman."

"But you didn't have a problem fucking with me when you found out I had a girl."

"Nigga, I didn't owe her loyalty. As her man, you did. As her man, all females should have been off limits and had no access to you in that way. You came to me on some business type shit and then started fucking me. We had been fucking around for a while until you told me you lived with your girl. You was already doing your dirt by then and I am pretty sure it's other bitches you was fucking with right along with me."

I couldn't even lie, the shit Azela was speaking was the truth. I owed Mizzy loyalty and I fucked that shit up. Despite how she found out, the shit should have never happened. I made it up in my mind that I was popping up over there today. This silent treatment shit was childish and we needed to have a serious conversation. I wasn't too proud to beg for my woman if that was what I had to do to

182

get us back on track.

"Fuck! I gotta get my shit together."

"Yeah, you do 'cause if you gon' stay here, you gotta pay."

"The fuck? Don't I already pay?"

"Yeah, you pay me for holding your shit here and risking my freedom. If you gon' be laying up in my shit, you gotta pay up, nigga. I got big bills."

"The fuck do you do with the money I give you?"

"Just like you just told me, stay out my business, nigga."

I grabbed my duffle bag that had the clothes and toiletries that I had to buy and headed toward the bathroom to take care of my hygiene. I thought about sending Mizzy a text to let her know I was coming over there, but I decided against it. Knowing her, if she knew I was coming, she would leave just to make sure she wouldn't have to face me. I was taking a risk by just popping up, but I prayed she would be there.

After finishing my hygiene, I made my way back into the kitchen where Azela was sitting. She looked so fucking good, if I wasn't already in a fucked-up situation, I would have had her ass stretched out across the table.

"I left my spare key on the coffee table in case you need it. I would never kick you while you are down, so I am willing to let you stay here for as long as you need to, but all I ask is that you take this DNA test for my son. Despite what you may think about me, I am a good mother and my son deserves to know who his father is. He didn't ask to be here. If the test proves you're not his father, then that's what it is, but I will say this; you are the only person I ever fucked raw. We didn't always use condoms, Ryan."

"Man, Azelae, this is the last thing I need on my plate right now, man."

"I'm not trying to complicate your life any more than it already is, but you made this bed and now you gotta lay in it."

"I don't have time for this right now. Thanks, but no thanks for the offer to stay."

I grabbed my keys and headed to my car. It was like bullshit was coming at me left and right. I knew there was a possibility that Azalea's baby could be mine, but that was the last thing I needed in my life. I wasn't ready to be a daddy. I knew it wasn't the child's fault, but right now, a DNA test was the least of my worries.

When they say a woman was a man's comfort and peace, that shit was real. I was completely lost without Mizzy right now. To say I was not nervous would be a lie. My palms were sweating and my heart was racing. Someone would swear I was sick with Covid from the way I was looking and breathing.

What normally took me about fifteen minutes turned into six minutes because I broke all types of traffic laws from speeding to running red lights. God was on my side because there was not a cop in sight. I made it to our condo, and thankfully, Mizzy's car was parked in her assigned parking spot. There was another car parked in the visitor spot where I usually parked. It was a car I had never seen so maybe it belonged to one of the other neighbors. I found a parking spot a few places down and parked. I wasn't a religious nigga, but I said a quick prayer before getting out of my car. The more I walked toward the door, the more

185

my hands started to sweat.

Finally making it to the door, I heard what seemed like a male voice and Mizzy both laughing and talking. I couldn't make out the voice, but the more I listened, the madder I got. Ain't no way she had a nigga in here and we had only been broken up for a few days. She couldn't answer my calls and texts but she could be laughing and talking to the next man.

I pulled out my key to let myself in. I needed to see who this nigga was in my house. Opening the door to the one place I called home, I was shocked to see JD sitting there, laughing all in my woman's face like they had known each other for years. How the hell did they know each other?

"Ryan, what are you doing here?"

"No, the question is, what are you doing in here with this nigga? How do you even know him? JD, what the fuck you doing here with my girl, nigga?"

"Wait, how do y'all know each other?"

"That don't matter. How do you know him, and why is he

186

in our house?"

"Our house? Ryan, I kicked you out. We broke up. I told you I was done with you so who I bring to my house, the house I pay bills at, the same house I was paying bills at before you moved in, is none of your business."

"Damn, JD, I thought females was a distraction? Ain't that the shit you always spitting? How the fuck you end up in my house with my girl?"

"Nah, my boy, you got things confused. She just said that y'all broke up and this is her house. My'Zariah invited me in."

"Man, fuck all that, Mizzy, can we please talk alone?"

"No, you need to leave, and leave my key before you go. We ain't got shit to talk about. I can have all of your shit packed in a day and drop it off at your place for you."

"So you choosing this nigga over me?"

"Ryan, I am not choosing anybody. I am done with you. You showed the ultimate disrespect by having a bitch in our house. Other females may give you a second chance after that shit, but not me. If I take you back, all I am doing is allowing you to continue to disrespect me, and I will be damned if I allow that."

"Mizzy, please, can we just talk? I don't care if it's over the phone, but don't give up on us."

"For the last time, Ryan, get out before I get my gun. You already know my aim is always on point."

"Fuck!" I yelled before turning around and heading out the door and back to my car. This trip was a bust. Shit had not turned out the way I prayed for them to. I was still trying to wrap my brain around how she knew JD. They seemed mighty close, to say they just met, but my gut was telling me they had known each other for a while now. She was pissed at me but I bet she was fucking around with this nigga the whole fucking time. They both were going to have to see me again and I put that on everything.

I drove away from the condo with a thousand and one thoughts running through my head. I needed to go and holler at Johntae to see what type of games he and his brother were on.

My'Zariah "Mizzy" Preston

"Ryan is your man?"

"No, he is my ex-man. How do y'all know each other, anyway?"

"He works for me."

"Wait, you're the one that he was saying was supposed to help him open his shop? What the fuck, man? It's like I can't get rid of this nigga."

"What you mean? I said he worked for me, I never said we were friends. I'm cool with the nigga because of what we

190

do out there in the streets, but I ain't never break bread with the nigga or no shit like that. I can't believe that nigga fumbled you, of all people. What was he thinking?"

"Thinking with his dick. So you know all about the hoes he was fucking with? Do you know the bitch he had in my house?"

"Nah, I don't, and if I did, it's not my place to tell you that. We not on no friendship level, but I ain't no snitching ass nigga, either."

"So you wouldn't tell me nothing about Ryan?"

"Nope, that's not how I want to start my relationship off with you. I'm trying to be in your future, not keep reminding you of your past. My goal is to help you heal from the shit the old nigga put you through, and how can you heal if the past is constantly being brought up? What sense does that make?"

"I understand, JD, but this shit just seems wrong."

"What's wrong about it? You asked if I knew him and I told you yes. I also told you how we knew each other. I

191

didn't lie about anything. I told you the truth, so there it is."

"So you don't feel no type of way about me dealing with him previously?"

"What is there to feel a way about? We weren't fucking when y'all were together. Look, My'Zariah, don't let your past blind you to what could be the future you have been looking for. I'm not tripping over that nigga and neither should you. I don't expect you to get over what y'all had so quickly—that would be selfish of me—but I can say I am trying to be here to help."

"I understand, but this is a lot to take in. I know Ryan and that nigga hates to lose. I just don't want there to be any beef between the two of y'all because of me."

"You don't have to worry about that. I would never beef with a nigga over something that's mine, and as far as Ryan trying me, he ain't that stupid."

"What was he talking about, girls being a distraction?"

"That was, and still is my motto. When it comes to these streets and making this money, you got to be focused. Any little distraction can cost you your life. With this type of lifestyle, you draw a lot of attention, especially from these females who are only looking for a come up. So I always say make the money your main focus, and once you're comfortable and ready to get out the game, then find your lady and live your life."

"So, you have never been in a relationship?"

"Not a serious one, no."

"So what am I? I am not trying to be a distraction. It's bad enough you know my ex."

"I wouldn't be here if I thought you were a distraction."

Looking at his lips while he spoke, I wanted nothing more than to kiss them. Before I could make my move, I felt his lips come crashing down against mine. For a man, he had some of the softest lips I had ever seen. The scent from his cologne was so inviting. I wrapped my arms around his neck as I stuck my tongue in his mouth. I could kiss him forever.

"You better stop kissing me like that."

193

"Why is that?"

"'Cause you're going to get something started that you're not ready to handle yet. Before I put this dick in your life, you got to make sure you and your ex are done. I don't share, and I am not about to go back and forth."

"I am done with Ryan. There is no more us, I swear."

"I hear you, baby girl, but it hasn't been that long, so to protect myself, I need to be sure that what y'all had is over. Plus, I just know that pussy is worth the wait."

"You say some of the wildest shit, Jadarius."

"The way you say my name sounds sexy as fuck. Make sure you say it just like that when I have you stretched out across my bed."

Oh my God, this man has no filter.

"You really don't care what comes out of your mouth, do you?"

"Nope, no need to sugarcoat shit. But let me get out of here, I got some business to handle. Make sure you answer when I call you tonight."

"I will." I walked JD to the door and watched as he pulled out of my visitor's parking space. Before going back in, I looked around the parking lot, making sure Ryan wasn't anywhere. Not seeing his car anywhere, I went back inside and made sure to lock my door, including the deadbolt that could only be locked from the inside. I didn't need him popping back up here. I decided I needed to get all of Ryan's things packed so he could get out of my house. I knew keeping his stuff here would just prolong the process of getting over him completely.

I didn't realize that packing his stuff would make me so emotional. I couldn't lie and say that I didn't love Ryan because I did, and still do. I overlooked a lot of shit because of my feelings for him. At one point, I envisioned Ryan and I married until I noticed all the changes in him. I tried to overlook shit but the last few months had really opened my eyes to the type of person he was.

It took me two hours to get all of his stuff packed. I didn't want anything left to keep reminding me of him.

195

A STREET KING TO LOVE

Jadarius (JD) White

Damn, I couldn't lie and say I wasn't shocked to find out that Mizzy was Ryan's girl. That shit was crazy because Mizzy was the full package and he cheated on her for these no-good broads in the street. What kind of shit was that nigga on? I knew he wasn't going to just sit back and watch his girl be with another nigga, but he didn't have a choice when it came to me and Mizzy. He didn't want her and he proved that by his actions.

Mizzy told me she found a pair of women's underwear in her bathroom and that was the ultimate disrespect. To bring a woman you fucking to the same place your main girl lays her head was a bitch move, in my opinion. The nigga was lucky I was not a petty motherfucker who would tell her everything I knew about him, but that was not my nature. Snitching on him would just keep reminding her of how much of a fuck boy he really was. I was a firm believer of

197

what happened in the dark would eventually come to the light. It would be just a matter of time before all his dirt would come out.

Dealing with Ryan was the least of my worries. I just couldn't get out of my head where I saw Mizzy's mama at before. When she approached us last night at the restaurant, her face seemed so familiar. I could tell from the tension that Mizzy didn't fuck with her birth mother like that at all, and from the way she was eye fucking me, I could tell she was no good. To say she was sick, she looked mighty healthy. Now, I am no expert on cancer or its symptoms, but the shit seemed off.

Tonight, I had to come to one of my warehouses to collect. This was usually the spot me, Ryan, and Johntae would meet. I wasn't expecting Ryan to show up, due to what went down at Mizzy's spot, but I prayed the nigga didn't play with my money. He wouldn't have to worry about beefing with me because he would no longer be able to walk on his own. I didn't play about my money and everyone who dealt with me knew that.

"JD, man, what is going on with you and Ryan? That nigga called my phone, talking about I was helping you take his girl. What the fuck."

I turned around and saw my brother walking toward me

198

with a blunt hanging from his lips. Of course, he was confused as to what was going on. I knew he wouldn't be left in the dark forever, but I didn't expect Ryan to go back, crying like a bitch.

"I see you have been talking to your right-hand man about me."

"Man, JD, what games are you playing? That nigga works for us, why you pushing up on his girl?"

"First off all, little brother, know all the facts before you come at me. I didn't take his girl from him; that dumb nigga fumbled that beautiful woman right to me, and that's just the facts."

"But how do you even know his girl? Is this the same girl you was talking about at your house the other day?"

"Yeah, but I didn't know that she was his girl."

"I am confused as fuck right now."

"Look, I met her down in Tennessee. She was down there with her brother. They both know Kari."

"So you stepped to her?

"Something like that."

"Man, this shit is crazy. JD, how can I work or be around that man if you fucking his girl?"

"Nah, nothing should interfere with your money. If he can't do his job, then you, as the boss, you know what you gotta do."

"What about the shop you trying to help him get?"

"I'm not stopping my money for no nigga. If he wants the shop, he has to come to me as a man so we can discuss it. I'm not going to stop him from getting his shop, but I am not going to beg him to fuck with me, either."

"Can you at least explain to me what the hell happened, JD? I don't like being left in the dark. Both of y'all my niggas but you're my big brother, so I'm going to always have your back."

I took a few moments to explain everything to Johntae. I even told him about our run-in at the mall. There was no need to hide and lie. Ryan fucked up and allowed another man to come in and take his woman. If he had to blame anyone, he needed to blame himself.

"Damn, JD, that nigga Ryan is a dumb nigga. I ain't never seen his girl, but from the way you talk about her, she bad."

"Ryan is a dummy. Not only is she beautiful, she's smart, too, and working on her own business."

"Sounds like you really feeling her, big brother."

"Yeah, I am."

"Well, you know I got your back with whatever. That nigga should have thought about the possibility of losing his girl when he was out there doing dirt."

"Exactly! Fucking dummy."

"Well, anyway, that nigga should be pulling up any minute, and I hope he ain't on no dumb shit."

"Fuck that nigga. As long as my money right, there will be no problems between us."

A few seconds later, Ryan walked into the warehouse, carrying his duffel bag. I was glad that nigga played it smart and didn't fuck with my money. As long as everything was there and accounted for, there would be no problems. I could tell he hated having to deal with me, but what the hell was he going to do about it? If he wanted out, oh well; he could easily be replaced.

"Here, Tae. It's all there and accounted for."

"Aight, bet. How much you trying to re-up?"

"The usual."

"Is there a reason you staring at me like that, nigga?"

202

I got tired of that nigga staring at me like he wanted these problems.

"JD, what the fuck? You supposed to be my boy. The minute you saw Mizzy was my bitch, you should have backed the fuck off and let us work out our problems."

"Nigga, I could see if y'all had simple problems, but man, you fucked up. How long was you going to cheat on her and not expect her to find out? I didn't know she was your girl until today. You pushed her away; it was going to be me or another nigga. She is done with you, so move on and let a nigga who gon' do her right, not fuck around on her, step in. And don't worry, all your dirt is safe with me. I wouldn't even tell her the dirt I know on you. My goal is to make her happy, inside and out, and when I do get the pussy, I will make sure she don't remember shit about you."

"Nigga, what?"

"Aye, Ryan, I suggest you think twice before you run up on my brother like that."

I glanced back at Tae as he walked toward Ryan and me, carrying the duffel bag full of product for Ryan.

"Damn, it's like that, Tae?"

"How do you expect it to be? That's my brother, my blood. You need to take this L and move around. You wanted to be playboy of the year and got sloppy and lost your girl, man. We got a business to run, and if you gon' be my right hand, you need to get your shit right. As long as you got beef with my brother, you got beef with me. So either you can get right or move around."

"Man, fuck this shit."

We watched as Ryan walked out of the warehouse, leaving his duffel bag behind. I didn't expect the nigga to leave money on the table like that but he did.

"Fuck, man. Now what the fuck am I gon' do? You about to be out and Pops is too fucking caught up with them damn strippers for anything."

"Tae, first thing, calm down. You don't know that he is not coming back. Let that man cool off, then give him a call and see where his head is at. If he not talking right, then we will figure something out. There will always be a Plan B, little brother, and you know I wouldn't leave you high and dry. You already know all the connects, along with all of their suppliers. Like you said, I taught you everything, you just got to have the confidence to keep the empire running. This is your show, now run it your way."

"Yeah, I know, JD, and I appreciate you, but I don't want you to put off everything you're trying to do with your business."

"You're not. Remember, I already for business up and running, so my cash flow comes in every month and I will get my gun shop real soon."

"Yeah, I know. Shit, it's just the two of us. Let's get started on running this money through the machines so we can get up out of here. I need a blunt and some pussy."

It took Tae and me another two hours before we had all the money counted up and stacked. All that was next was to contact our connect to get more product and continue with business as usual.

"Aight, little brother. I'm headed to the house and crashing.

I am dog tired. I'm gon' holla at you tomorrow."

I dapped my brother up and headed to my car. I didn't
realize how hungry I was until I heard my stomach growl. I
decided to stop at everyone's favorite hood restaurant,
Waffle House. I fucked with their all-star breakfast heavy
and that was exactly what I wanted.

Pulling up in the parking lot, I noticed what looked like
Ryan's car. Getting closer, I saw it was Ryan's car and he
stood on the side, arguing with a female. Curiosity got the
best of me and I was curious who he was arguing with. I
put my window down just enough to hear the conversation.
Damn, this was the woman who left her underwear at
Mizzy's house. I heard them arguing about how she set him
up. Damn, she didn't have a care in the world about what
she had done. I really wanted to see who this woman was.
When she finally turned around, I kicked myself for being
so nosey. I knew this man was not fucking with her. I
instantly got pissed off. How stupid could this nigga be?
Then I realized where I had seen Mizzy's mother. It was at
one of the trap houses and this nigga was dicking her down.
He had to know who she was to Mizzy. I knew if Mizzy
found this shit out, it would hurt her even more. This nigga
was a straight up fucking clown.

My appetite was gone. I just wanted to go home and figure
this shit out.

Keon "Ke" Preston

I took my sister up on her advice and reached out to Malik. Like she said, we had too much history to not figure out where we were in our relationship. I asked him to come over because I didn't think we needed to be in public. Malik still had his key, so I heard when he walked through the door. Damn, just like always, he looked so good. Good enough to eat. I had to remember why he was here. Lord knows I loved this man with everything in me and I prayed we could come to some kind of common ground within our relationship.

"Hey."

"What's up, how you doing?"

"I'm doing as good as can be expected, Malik."

His nonchalant attitude was starting to really piss me off. He was really acting like we weren't going through shit.

"Malik, what's really going on? You got this I don't care attitude. What are we doing?"

"Keon, you walked out on me, not the other way around. I was just trying to explain how I was feeling, and like you always do, you blew up."

"You basically said that you were embarrassed by me and what I choose to do with my life. How would you feel if I said that about you and your career? I love makeup and I am good at it. I help people feel beautiful and I am proud. I may not help them legally like you, but I still help them, and you being embarrassed by that is unacceptable to me."

"I never said you were an embarrassment, Keon. I know how much you love what you do. If it came out that way, I'm sorry, but the real issue with us is that you want me to be completely out with my sexuality, and I can't do that right now. I have a reputation at my job I need to uphold and I don't need my colleagues to know I am gay. That's just something I am not ready for. I want to move up in the company and I don't want that lingering over my head, not right now."

"OK, so when? You expect me just to keep waiting for you to find your identity. Is that what you're saying? You want me to just wait around until it's safe for you to come play house with me? I'm not doing that anymore. I feel like you have hidden me from your life since we been together. You have met all of my family and I have never met yours. What kind of mess is that?"

"This has nothing to do with my family, this is between me and you."

"You know, for someone in the legal profession, you really act stupid sometimes. This has nothing to do with your family, this is between me and you and our relationship. We are in 2023; gay couples come out all the time, famous or not. Hell, some of your coworkers are probably just as gay as you and as feminine as me, so what you saying is a weak ass excuse. I am too fine to be hidden from the world. I am a good person. I not only treat others right but I treat you right. You want to hide me from the world but you don't mind having me suck your dick or bend over. I feel like a side bitch."

"You are not a side bitch, Keon. Never have been."

"Then what am I? What are we?"

"Keon, I need to figure some shit out."

"OK, but don't expect me to sit around like a sitting duck, waiting for you to figure it out."

"What is that supposed to mean?"

"That means, as of now, I am free to do as I please and date who I please. I refuse to wait around for you to figure shit out."

"Keon, just give me some time, please."

"I have given you nothing but time, Malik. I am all out."

"Don't give up on me."

"I haven't given up, you are."

I was proud of myself for standing my ground. I wanted to break down and cry so bad, but I refused to let him see me cry. I loved me more and I was pushing away a man who really liked me and holding my life back.

"Keon, please, just give me some time. That's all I ask, baby."

"How much time, Malik?"

"I don't know, but despite how you feel, I love you."

"I love you, too, Malik, but I won't wait forever for you to decide what you want to do."

"I understand."

I watched as Malik got up to leave. I wanted to stop him, but I couldn't let him see me break. Once the door was closed, all my emotions spilled out and all the tears I fought so hard to hold back cascaded down my face. A good cry was all I needed. I got myself together and was ready to take on the day. I was finally ready to take Zakari up on his offer to go to dinner with him. Waiting around for someone who wasn't comfortable within themselves, I was good on him.

My'Zariah "Mizzy" Preston

For the past few days, the us have been going pretty well. I had been spending a lot of time with JD and he was a man of his word and was helping with all of my plans and ideas. We had a few more dates, and with each one, I was beginning to like him more and more. He was not only a very smart man, but he was funny as hell and he kept me laughing. Today, he was taking me to look at a few buildings for my first event store front. In my plan, I decided to open the first one in Charlotte. I didn't want anything too big just to get started.

"The first building we looked at was the nicest one, and it was in a great location and neighborhood."

"Is that the one you want?"

"Yeah, I think that is the one."

"Well, tomorrow, we can speak with the realty company and talk numbers."

"We?"

"Yeah, this is your first business; you don't want them to try to fuck you over."

"I would appreciate that."

"No problem. Are you hungry?"

"OK, let's go get something to eat before your last class."

Something JD and I were doing that Ryan and I never did was build a friendship. We were getting to know each other on a more intimate level. Not once had he forced me into sex or anything. The attraction was there and the sexual tension was thick and I was fighting it, but I was enjoying spending so much time with him.

Being that I didn't have a lot of time before I had to be back in class, I really wanted something quick, so we pulled up to Burger King.

"You heard from that clown Ryan lately?"

"Nope. I texted him to come and get his shit but he never responded. Oh well, the shit will end up in the trash for all I care."

"Do what you gotta do. This drive-thru line is long, let's go inside."

Walking inside wasn't any better than being in the line. They were still slow as hell and we still ended up waiting to order. After a fifteen minute wait, we were finally getting our food and walking to a table.

"What's up, JD?"

"What's good, Azalea?"

"My money is running low, where that nigga Ryan at?"

"How do you know Ryan?" I had to ask. I wanted to know if this was the bitch that was in my house.

"Mizzy, drop it, love."

"You're Mizzy?"

"And who are you?"

"I'm Azalea, Ryan's baby mama, but I'm not the one who was in your house. That was someone a lot closer to you than you think."

"Azalea, get the fuck on now. I don't know where that nigga at, and whatever situation y'all got ain't got shit to do with me."

"You just tell that nigga my money running low. We got a deal."

I couldn't catch a damn break. Shit was always being

thrown at me. This nigga had a whole baby on me. I wasn't even hungry anymore and damn sure didn't feel like going back to class.

"You knew about the baby?"

"I knew there was a possibility that her baby could be his, but that bitch fucks around, so it could be from anyone."

"And you couldn't tell me that?"

"Like I told you before, it's not my place to tell that man's business."

"I get that, but that man was out there raw dogging all types of bitches. I need to get checked out."

"We can go together."

"You would do that with me?"

"Yeah, we might as well start our relationship off with a

clean bill of health."

"Damn, no one has ever done nothing like that for me before."

"It's not a nigga around like me."

"Just answer one question for me, please."

"I will try."

"Do you know who was in my house? She said it was someone close to me."

"Look, baby girl, what I am about to tell you is something I think you should know. I am going against my word, but I can't let this hang over my head. The other night, when your sister and birth mother came over to us, I didn't say anything because I kept trying to remember where I knew her from. I couldn't remember until the other night when me and Ryan had some words and he left out. A few hours later, I left and went to get some food. I saw Ryan and some woman arguing outside of the restaurant. Curiosity got the best of me and I waited to see who she was. I heard them arguing about her being in your house and he said she set him up. Mizzy, it was your birth mother. That nigga was fucking with her. Seeing them together, I remembered seeing her at one of my trap houses. Damn, man, this is some shit you shouldn't have to deal with."

"Take me to my car, please."

"You OK to drive? I can take you where you need to go. If you don't want to go to class, I can take you home and we can chill over there."

"I'm not going home. Take me to my parents's house. I will give you the address."

How could they do this to me? I was so tired of people fucking over me. People often called me mean but I was fed up. I didn't know why Mellissa hated me so much. It wasn't like I asked to be here; she made that choice. As hard as I tried to fight it, I couldn't help the tears from falling. What did I do to get hurt like this?

"Don't cry, Mizzy. I know you're hurt, but my job is to protect you and keep you from being hurt. I promise you, as long as I am in your life, you won't ever have to cry."

"I don't understand what I did so bad to deserve this."

"You didn't deserve this. That nigga Ryan is a fuck boy. I don't know the deal with your birth mother but Ryan doesn't deserve any more of your tears, so make this the last day you cry over that nigga."

I was glad to see that all of my siblings and Mellissa were at my parents's house when we pulled up. I needed them to hear this as well.

"Mizzy Miz, what's up, baby sis?"

"Where is Mellissa, Melo?"

"In there with Mama and Akron. What's wrong?"

"I'm about to kill that bitch."

I stormed through my parents's house in search of the one person I hated the most. I didn't even realize JD was still behind me. I walked into the kitchen and my eyes landed on Mellissa. Something took over me and I attacked.

"You nasty ass bitch! You was in my house, fucking my boyfriend? What the hell did I ever do to you?"

I blacked out on Mellissa. All the anger I'd held on to for over twenty years came out at this very moment. I didn't come to until I felt JD's arms grab me and hold me back. My grandparents and siblings all looked shook. I had done a number on Mellissa. Her lip was bleeding and her eye was beginning to swell, and still, I felt like that wasn't enough.

"Mizzy, what are you doing, sis? What happened?"

"Ask this bitch what happened. Ask her why she was in my house with Ryan's sad ass. Ask her why her dirty draws were left in my bathroom. This nasty bitch hates me so much, she would stoop that low. I didn't ask to come into this world, yet she treats me like I'm the enemy."

"Mellissa, I know you didn't!" Keon yelled while removing his earrings, which meant only one thing: he was getting ready to fight. But I didn't need him to help me fight. I could handle this bitch on my own.

"Fuck you, Mizzy. All you are is a spoiled little bitch. I never wanted kids and I never liked you. I wanted to give you to foster care because I didn't want to have to look at your face. That's why I left."

"Then why are you here? I never asked you to come here and spend time with me. I never asked you to be a mother to me. I never wanted nothing from you, not a relationship, not shit. Yet, you come here and make it your duty to try to break me. This time, you crossed the line, and if you are sick with cancer, I hope that shit makes you suffer before it takes you out."

"My'Zariah!"

"I'm sorry, Mama, but your daughter is a fucked-up individual. She hates me so much, but she was the one popping pussy at sixteen and got pregnant. So what was it? The nigga you really wanted to be my daddy wasn't, so he stopped fucking with you? Is that why you hate me so much? Is that what it is? You come back in town and everybody can see right through you except me and Keon. You don't care about nobody but yourself. Oh, and tell everybody you are a dope fiend. That's what Ryan was giving you in exchange for sex, right? Dope. What are you, broke?"

"I don't have to explain nothing to you, you ungrateful bitch. And no, I'm not sick, I just wanted to fuck with you. Ryan was an added bonus, but no worries, I didn't fuck him, just gave him some award-winning head that he couldn't get enough of."

"Ohhh, you a nasty bitch!" I heard Keon yell.

"Yeah, she is a nasty bitch, and before I end up in jail for killing this bitch, I will leave. Mama and Daddy, as long as she is here, I will not step back in this house 'cause next time, I just might take her life."

And with that, I headed back out toward JD's car, with him right behind me. This was a side of me I never wanted him to see, but it is what it is.

"Do you know where I can find Ryan? I want his shit out of my house before I burn it. I am done with both of their asses."

"Don't worry about Ryan, I can handle him. I'm taking you to my house for a while so you can calm down, Killa."

"Thank you." I rested my head on the back of the headrest and closed my eyes, letting the wind hit me in the face. If I never saw Mellissa again, it would be too soon.

Jadarius (JD) White

I sat at my desk and watched Mizzy. I had only known her for a few weeks and I could tell she had been through a lot. Her birth mother was a foul ass bitch and that ass whipping Mizzy put on her earlier wasn't enough. She deserved a lot more and Ryan was next on her list and I was going to make it happen. I wanted her to be the one to tell him she knew everything and whatever she wanted to do, then I would be sure to make it happen.

First, I was going to make sure he never found work in North Carolina again. That nigga was foul and he needed to suffer for how he did my girl. I sent Johntae a text, telling him and Ryan to pull up. I knew it would be a shot in the dark but I told Tae to do whatever he had to. I had just received a text from Tae, telling me they were ten minutes away. I didn't want to wake her up, but we needed to get this over with.

"Baby girl, wake up." I slightly nudged her, waking her from her sleep.

"How long have I been sleep?"

"A few hours."

"I need to get my car and go home."

"I'll take you to do all of that, but first, we have to handle something."

"What?"

"You said you wanted to have a conversation with your ex, right?"

"No, I want to beat his ass like I did that bitch."

"OK, if that's what you want."

"What?"

"Him and my brother are on their way here."

"Are you serious?"

"Have I lied to you yet?"

"No."

"Aight, let's go downstairs, they should be pulling up in a minute."

We walked downstairs just as I saw my brother's car was pulling up to my house. I glanced over at Mizzy and she had this look on her face that tore at my heart. Her face held so much hurt and pain and that shit made me hurt.

Mizzy held on tight to my hand as we watched Ryan and Tae walkup to my front door. Tae didn't have a clue what was going on.

As soon as the door opened and Ryan walked through the door, Mizzy let go of my hand, ran right toward Ryan, and slapped his ass so hard, I felt that shit. The slap caught him off guard and he almost fell on his ass.

"You a nasty ass nigga, Ryan. My birth mother? You let that bitch suck your dick for dope, and you got a baby. You lucky I love my freedom and I didn't blow your fucking head off like I wanted to, but you're not worth it. I don't ever want to see you again. If I see you again, I might just kill you."

I waited for Mizzy to go back upstairs before I said what I needed to say to Ryan. My girl never wanted to see him again, so I was making it happen.

"You already lost your spot on this team, so don't even think about it. In the few weeks I have known Mizzy, I have developed strong feelings for her as a friend and as my girl. The shit she went through today could have been avoided, had you listened to me and kept your head on straight, make your money and get your shop open, but you wanted to be playboy of the year and it cost you your job, girl, and so much more. So this is where we at. She said she never wants to see you again, so you're going to leave town tonight. I don't give a fuck where you go, just fucking leave. Whatever money you got, keep it, but make sure you are out of Charlotte—hell, out of the south. Tae, make sure this fuck boy gets to the nearest state line."

I didn't even wait for them to leave before I turned around and headed up to my girl. Like it or not, Mizzy was mine. I was feeling her a lot and we hadn't even had sex yet. Just from our time together, I could see that she always had to be so hard, but now, she would be able to focus on her school and her career. I was new at this relationship thing, but for my first time, I think I got it right. Truth was, I had always been afraid of love, but it took a strange encounter for me to meet the person I wanted to experience my first and hopefully last relationship with.

EPILOGUE

Two Years Later

"Ohhh, Mizzy, bitch, that ring is nice. That's some Jacob the Jeweler type shit here. And look at the bling on my goddaughter. I am so happy for you."

"Thank you, Keon."

It had been two years and JD had finally asked me to marry him. Our daughter, Mariah, had just turned one and she was the light of our lives. She was definitely a surprise to us all. In the last two years, in addition to our daughter, JD and I both had our businesses up and running. JD finally got his gun shop opened, along with the gun range, and I had two event company locations: one in Charlotte and one in Tennessee. I thought it would only be right to have a company in the same state as my man. We would often spend time between the two.

When I met JD, I was dealing with a lot and I often felt broken, but I was so used to always having to be so strong that was all I knew, but with JD, he let me be me. If I needed to cry, he was right there, giving me his shoulder to lean on. Our relationship was one I'd always prayed for. For JD, this was his first real relationship and that man treated me like a queen. He always said that he was never taught to properly love a woman, but he was learning as we went. I was so proud of my man. Not only did he have multiple businesses but he was a great father to our daughter. He had her so spoiled that often, no one could keep her because all she did was cry for him.

Keon was still his overly extra self and he and Zakari had been together for a little over a year. He got tired of waiting on Malik and finally decided to give Zakari a chance and they had been together since. JD did end up giving Kari the building in Tennessee and he also had his studio up and running and of course, he had the baddest makeup artist on his arm. Zakari wasn't ashamed of Keon and loved to show him off and that was all my brother wanted: somebody to be proud to have him on their arm.

As far as Mellissa, just like always, she was in and out of town, but she made sure to stay clear of me. My grandparents made it clear that if she was in town, she could not come to their house out of respect for me. To be honest, the only one who still fucked with her was Kelsey. I loved my sister but I learned a long time ago that she was a little slow. If she wanted to keep being used, that was on her. I washed my hands of it.

"You know I love you, right, Mizzy?"

"Yes, JD. I love you, too, baby."

"You have made me a happy man and I can't thank you enough for giving me something I was afraid of."

"What was that?"

"Real love. Real Black love."

"Awww, baby, you have made me just as happy. You helped to heal me after so much hurt and I am forever grateful for you."

"Enough of all this mushy shit. Let's send Mariah home with her god daddies so we can work on her brother."

"How do you know they want to keep her tonight?"

231

"Because I already talked to them and you have to cook them dinner on Sunday."

"What?"

"That's what they wanted, baby, and Mariah's bag is already packed."

"JD, you had this planned out?"

"Sure did, now come on so I can beat that pussy up the way you like it."

"Damn, my man, my man, my man!"

JAMIE MARIE

A STREET KING TO LOVE

Made in the USA
Middletown, DE
05 July 2023

34598439R00136